DEATH SAILS
THE NILE

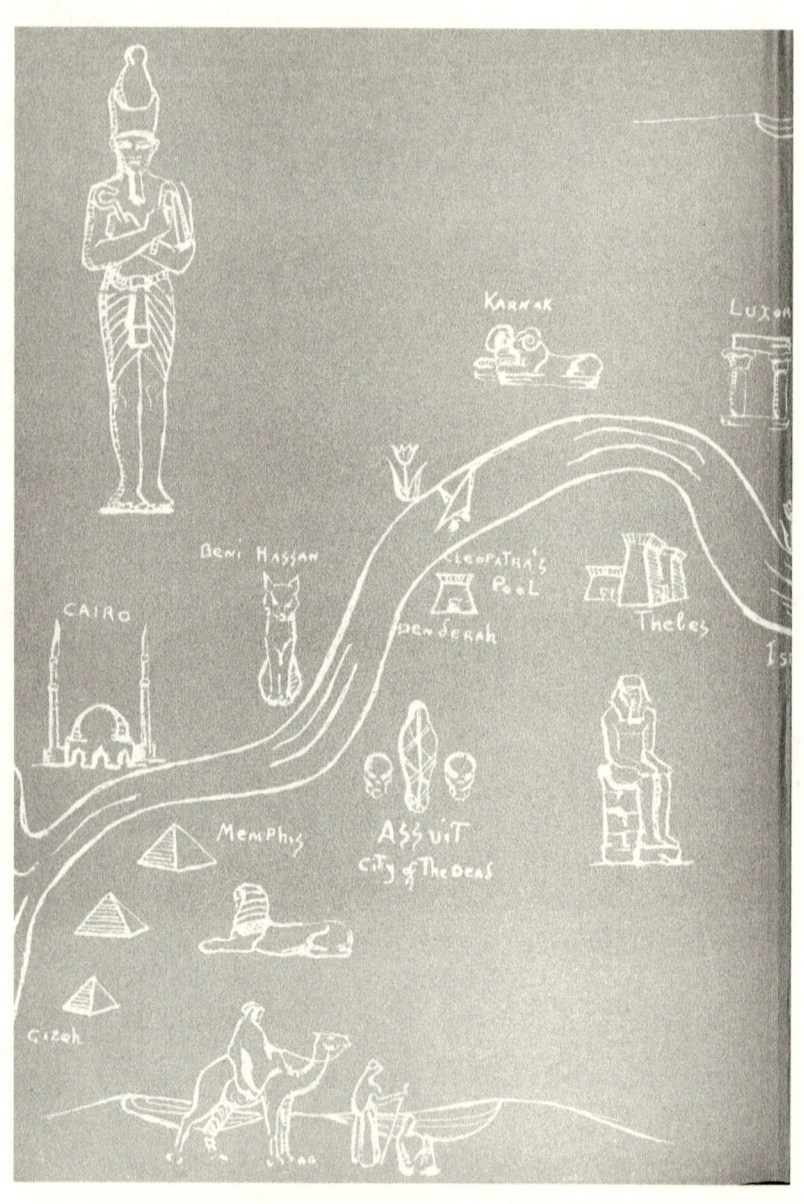

ENDPAPER DESIGN BY MARIE AGNES BENOIST, DAUGHTER
OF AGNES FOY BENOIST (SEE INSCRIPTION, NEXT PAGE)

To Agnes Fay Benoist who is always gracious clever and beautiful.

F. Burke McKinley

AUTHOR'S INSCRIPTION WITHIN
A COPY OF *DEATH SAILS THE NILE*

DEATH SAILS
THE NILE

F. Burks McKinley

COACHWHIP PUBLICATIONS
Greenville, Ohio

Death Sails the Nile, by F. Burks McKinley
© 2018 Coachwhip Publications

Frances Burks McKinley (1907-1970)
Published 1933
No claims made on public domain material.
Introduction © Curtis Evans
Cover image: Horned viper © Matthijs Kuijpers
Title page: A 'modern steam-dahabeah' on the Nile, 1904

CoachwhipBooks.com

ISBN 1-61646-454-2
ISBN-13 978-1-61646-454-7

THE NILE AIN'T JUST A MYSTERY BY CHRISTIE
DEATH SAILS THE NILE (1933)
AND THE LIFE JOURNEY OF FRANCES BURKS

CURTIS EVANS

Because everything she wrote gets remembered—and her writing typically is rather memorable indeed to mystery fans—Agatha Christie often is assumed invariably to have been a crime fiction originator. Often she was, but sometimes she was not. We find an instance of the latter case—where she was not—with her classic detective novel *Death on the Nile* (1937), wherein her great Belgian sleuth, Hercule Poirot, confronts a murderous ménage of devious European and American sophisticates on a tour boat in Egypt. The novel was not in fact, as is generally believed, the first Nile River cruise mystery. In novel form, anyway, that distinction would appear to belong to *Death Sails the Nile*, a detective novel published four years earlier by American author F. Burks McKinley.[1] *Death Sails the Nile* was well-received by critics, with the *Saturday Review*, for example, pronouncing the novel "good" and explicating: "Authentic Egyptian background succeeds in producing unique atmosphere of terror. Plenty of clues and strange occurrences." Yet until its reissuance this year by Coachwhip, the novel had been out-of-print for 85 years, with the author evidently having abandoned for good and all her stated intention of launching a mystery-writing career.

Her—yes, the person hidden behind the androgynous name of F. Burks McKinley was Mary Frances Burks McKinley, who at the time of the publication of her sole mystery novel was merely 26 years old, a recent college graduate and near newlywed. The only daughter of James Willis Burks and Linnie Mai Atkins, the author was born Mary Frances Burks on November 24, 1907, at the farm of her maternal grandfather Asa Allen Atkins (formerly part of her great grandfather James Atkins' 800-acre tobacco plantation), near the small town of Newbern in Dyer County, a "severely conservative" (to quote a recent presidential candidate) corner of northwestern Tennessee. At the county seat, Dyersburg, a Confederate memorial had been erected on the grounds of the courthouse in 1905, two years before Frances' birth, on the 43rd anniversary of the Battle of Shiloh. A dozen years later the stone rebel soldier that stood impassively at the top of the memorial looked on, along with thousands of vocal flesh-and-bone citizens of Dyer County, as Lation Scott, a black man accused of raping a white woman, was brutally tortured with red hot pokers for several hours before finally being incinerated at an impromptu stake. "It was the biggest thing since Ringling Brothers' Circus came to town," one eyewitness later recalled with gusto.[2] Perhaps some of the onlookers and/or participants at Lation Scott's ghastly lynching just over a century ago were among those who had been "saved" at massive religious revivals conducted in the county in 1904 and 1907. In any event, Mary Frances Burks in her own life left the strangely mingled savagery and sanctimony of the Jim Crow-era South far behind her, eventually attaining heights known only, in both her day and in ours, to a fortunate few.

Frances's father, James Willis Burks, came from another rural Tennessee county, Overton, located in north central Tennessee. Educated at Livingston Academy in Livingston, the county seat of Overton, and at Draughon's Business College in Nashville, the capital of Tennessee, Burks became a druggist and served in the National Guard. Over a period of two decades he saw action in the Spanish-American War, the Philippine-American War, the so-called Pancho Villa Expedition and the First World War, rising to the rank of Major and receiving the Medal of Honor. During this time the peripatetic Burks ran drugstores in Livingston and Nashville, Little Rock, Arkansas, and Toledo, Ohio, where his and Linnie Mai's only other child, James Willis Burks III, was born in 1911. Frances and her brother spent their adolescent years mostly in Livingston, where their father and grandfather, Robert Lee Burks (a Civil War veteran, eulogist of the "lost cause," ardent prohibitionist, and devoted member of the Christian Church), owned the Burks Drug Company on the courthouse square, and in Nashville, where the Burks family moved in 1920, when Frances was twelve years old.

After graduating in 1925 from Nashville's Hume-Fogg High School, where she played on the girls' basketball team, Frances matriculated at Vanderbilt University, where she joined Tri Delta

Classical Club

Top Row—Webb, Battle, Brown, Neel, Burks
Bottom Row—Bransford, Evans, Kirk, Lipscomb

Y. W. C. A. Cabinet

sorority and majored in Classics. A 1927 photo of Vanderbilt's Classical Club, organized to promote the study of Latin and Greek, shows a nineteen-year-old Frances looking forthrightly at the camera, attractive and boyish-looking in a dark dress with checkered belt and collar and a fawn coat and her arm about the shoulder of another young woman. On the same day that she received her BA degree, June 12, 1929, she wed the socially prominent Silas Bent McKinley, a 35-year-old graduate of Harvard University (where he had been a member of the Hasty Pudding) and assistant professor of history at Vanderbilt and a nephew of noted journalist and author Silas Bent. (Among McKinley's distinguished ancestors were Kentucky senator and US Attorney General John J. Crittenden and Alabama senator and US Supreme Court Justice John McKinley.) Frances had proven a highly promising scholar at Vanderbilt, having been awarded the Founder's Medal as the top graduating student in the College of Arts and Sciences and served as an assistant to Professor Clyde Pharr, the noted head of the Classics Department, in Pharr's landmark translation of the Codex Theodosianus (Theodosian Code).[3] However, after receiving an MA degree at Vanderbilt in October 1930—her thesis was on Cicero's essay *Cato Maior de Senectute* (*On Old Age*)—Frances left Vanderbilt and moved with her husband, who had accepted a position at Washington University, to live in an opulent $75,000 mansion (about $1,135,000 today) in the wealthy enclave of Brentmoor Park, Clayton, a suburb of Saint Louis.

While living in the lap of luxury in Brentmoor Park, where the newlywed couple enjoyed the services of a chauffeur and cook, Frances in November 1933 published what turned out to be her only mystery, *Death Sails the Nile*, for the writing of which she drew upon her experiences in Egypt during the three-and-a-half-month Mediterranean honeymoon idyll she had enjoyed with her husband. Frances dedicated the novel, which was handsomely produced by an interesting Boston publisher, The Stratford Company, to Silas (though she is referred to as "Miss McKinley" on the back cover) and had the endpapers illustrated with an Egyptian motif by a talented friend, Marie Agnes Benoist (1907-1968), whose acquaintance she had recently made.[4] Agnes Benoist, an independently wealthy dilettante artist and sculptor, was one of the many grandchildren of one of 19th century Saint Louis's wealthiest and most important citizens, banker and financier Louis Auguste Benoist. Not only did Agnes design the endpapers for Frances's book, she also executed the murals in two of the bathrooms at Frances's house at Brentmoor Park. Downstairs bright blue and red ships sailed upon a deep blue sea while upstairs planets majestically glittered.

Just as Frances' relationship with Agnes was taking sail, however, her marriage with Silas was foundering. The husband-and-wife's holiday cruise to the West Indies in December 1934, during which Frances had planned to work on another mystery, was beset with acrimony, as Silas demanded a divorce from his wife. Informing Frances upon their return to St. Louis that he could no longer live happily in the same house with her, Silas left Brentmoor Park a few days after Christmas, declaring that he would never return to reside with his lawfully wedded wife. In January 1935, Frances thereupon sued Silas for divorce, alleging "general indignities" and asking for alimony and a return of her maiden name.

Frances's suit, which made national headlines in an era when divorce could still be considered shocking ("Woman Writer of Mystery Tales Sues for Divorce"), was quickly granted; and in March, while her now ex-husband Silas wed another woman, Frances traveled to the island of Bermuda for a two-week stay with her friend Agnes. That same year, she took up residence in her and Silas' apartment overlooking Central Park (now the site of the Park Lane Hotel), informing newspapers that she planned to take up journalism. There in 1940 she was still residing, along with Agnes, although she seems to have abandoned journalism as a possible profession. In 1943 she again enrolled, at the age of 35, at Vanderbilt University, registering for four classes, but she withdrew after only a couple of months. In the end Frances' life—which ended on September 5, 1970, at a house far from Tennessee in the historic Spanish-American city of Antigua, Guatemala, which Agnes, who had died two years earlier, used to visit—seems to have consisted of a series of false, if promising, starts, with much potential sadly left unrealized.

****

In 1937, two years after her divorce from Silas McKinley, Frances hosted, at her Central Park abode, a wedding reception for her 26-year-old brother James Willis Burks III, a Vanderbilt graduate and student at Washington University School of Medicine (he had earlier dropped out of Virginia Military Institute, rejecting his father's martial way of life), and alluring chanteuse Alice Weaver, daughter of a locomotive engineer from Carbondale, Illinois, and a former vocal teacher at the Fanchon and Marco School of the Theater in Hollywood, California. The songstress likely had caught Burks' eye at the Hotel Kingsway tavern in St. Louis, where, it was chattily confided in the St. Louis *Star and Times*, the "lovely and gracious doll" had performed an engagement with "he-man pianist" Herme Zinzer. In 1945, after a stint in the army during the Second World War, the younger Burks received an MSc degree in dermatology and syphilology from the University of Minnesota Graduate School of Medicine. Although his wife Alice sued him for divorce two years later, after a decade of marriage and the birth of a daughter, Mary Frances, who was named after his sister, his professional life flourished, as he became professor of clinical medicine in dermatology at Tulane University School of Medicine. He later married a second time, to Alma Rita Limberg, a New Orleans native 16 years younger than he, and with her fathered a boy and a girl.

In 1961, a year after the birth of his son and namesake James Willis Burks IV, Dr. Burks delivered a paper at the annual Academy of Dermatology and Syphilology Symposium in Therapy held at Chicago, Illinois. He opened his speech by wryly recalling a "pessimistic, dyspeptic colleague-in-training" from the 'Forties who had been dismayed by all the advances being made in medicine, which the colleague believed would destroy the medical practice by making disease obsolete:

> He pointed out that half of our practice had already
> disappeared. Hopes for survival dimmed though

the years every time I heard from him . . . the only
things remaining for us to treat would be acne and
ringworm. Since griseofulvin (a medication used to
treat ringworm) has appeared, I have not had the
heart to speak to him. I sincerely hope he is spared
the knowledge of the monumental breakthrough in
therapeutics I will reveal in the latter part of this
presentation.

Dr. Burks died in 1978, not long before his son Jamie enrolled at Tulane University. After his graduation from Tulane
in 1982, Jamie worked as a model in Europe and attended graduate school at UCLA. He was living in Los Angeles when he was
hospitalized for complications from AIDS, from which he died,
at the age of 34, on November 7, 1994, seventeen days before
what would have been his Aunt Frances' 87th birthday. Jamie was
interred in the Burks family tomb at Metairie Cemetery in New
Orleans, where his father and Frances had already been laid to
rest. Mourners were urged to make memorial contributions to the
fight against AIDS, a scourge which Dr. Burks' dyspeptic colleague
in dermatology and syphilology should have found highly grat-
ifying, as the treatment of it presented dilemmas indeed for the
medical specialist. A college photo of a nineteen-year-old Jamie Burks
can be found on Instagram's *The Aids Memorial*, where Jamie is one
among thousands of posted casualties of the dread disease. At the
site Jamie's tragically foreshortened life of passion and promise is
given moving remembrance by his friend Jonathan Taylor:

> Jamie and I met in New York, 1981. Kappa Sigma
> photo shows him in college—a snapshot I kept from
> his belongings (he would be very embarrassed by
> this image). Jamie, pictured right, the funniest,
> silliest crazy boy and man. The sweetest face. The
> best laugh—gasping for air, nearly silent in disbe-
> lief, tears streaming down our faces with laughter.
> How I remember him. A great friend I miss terribly.

Jamie's sad passing contrasted with his brief, wonderful life, 1960-1994.

Certainly the Burks family, from Frances and her brother James
to her nephew Jamie, seem to have lived lives that were relatively
freed from the traditional constraints of the rural South, with all
the pinnacles and pitfalls which such untethered lives entail. In
Frances' case she left mystery fans, amid an unfortunate litter
of false starts and dead ends, a fine detective novel to enjoy, now
reissued 85 years after its original publication.

DEATH SAILS THE NILE (1933)

*Miss Singlefoot was dressed for dinner. She made a
point of it while traveling. She never had a chance
at home. That was the nice thing about English
boats. People always dressed for dinner on them.
Come storms, come groundings, come murders, the
entire passenger list was found in evening clothes
by seven o'clock.*

—*Death Sails the Nile*, by
Frances Burks McKinley

During her leisurely 1929 Mediterranean honeymoon with her
new husband, Vanderbilt history professor Silas Bent McKinley,
Frances Burks with Silas visited the Egyptian city of Luxor, where,
in addition to seeing some of the greatest antiquities known to man-
kind, the couple encountered that "Lord of Reptiles" and veritable
"King of Wizards," Sheikh Moussa (or Musa, which is Arabic for
Moses), who was then the most renowned of Egypt's fabled snake
charmers. Four years later, when writing her detective novel *Death
Sails the Nile*, Frances placed Moussa/Musa, his name changed to
"Nusa," in the first chapter of the novel. There he is overheard by
newspaperwoman Mona Case and her young shipboard pal Jimmie
Bean, both of whom are passengers on the Nile River dahabeah

(tour boat) *Assuit*, in the act of presenting an unknown person with a baneful gift of two deadly asps. Is it a coincidence, then, when, on the very next day, another passenger on the boat, glamorous ash blonde Celia Lawton—"a magnet that attracted to its dynamic center every male eye within range, and every woman's too, for that matter"—suddenly crumples and dies, while standing before an image of Anubis, dread Egyptian god of the afterlife, at the ancient Abu Simbel temple complex, the victim (like, legend tells us, Cleopatra before her) *of a fatal bite from an asp*? You surely already know the answer to this question, dear readers!

A 1936 Newspaper Feature Noting Sheikh Moussa

Thus begins a reign of terror aboard *Assuit* that ultimately will claim three more lives before the ill-fated dahabeah reaches the protection afforded by modern civilization's gendarmerie. Besides Mona and Jimmie and the late Celia Lawton, the boat's other Europeans and Americans (this being a Golden age mystery, the Arab crew is considered, to borrow John Dickson Carr's apt phrase, "below suspicion") are the rotund medico and captain, Dr. Bradshaw, and the remaining surviving passengers. These are Professor Cross, an acerbic archaeologist; Jack Spencer, a devilishly charming man-of-the-world; Ella Singlefoot, Mona's primly outspoken spinster aunt; Tom Amory, a hulking engineer said to have been, up until her ghastly untimely death, Celia's fiancée; Colonel Worthington, late of the British Army, and his wife, Sophie, formerly a chorus girl in the Ziegfeld Follies; and Celia's plain Jane maid, Jane Davet. Who among them will be dastardly done to death before intrepid Mona Case discovers both a motive and a murderer?

Readers who have perused the biographical portion of this introduction may perceive some similarity between Mona Case and the author. Not only is 25-year-old Mona Case the same age as Frances Burks when she was writing the novel, she bears a physical resemblance to her as well and seems in some ways a fantasy projection: a person who chose the life of an independent career woman, which the author herself foreswore when she married Silas Bent McKinley. It will be recalled that after her divorce from Silas, Frances talked of becoming a journalist. She tellingly describes Mona as follows:

> Twenty-five years of active and strenuous American life had given Mona Case unusual poise and an air of assurance. In four years after leaving college she had established a definite place for herself in the newspaper world. . . . She was of medium height, slender, with a mass of short auburn curls topping a well-shaped head. She combined in her person the qualities of physical strength and vivacious charm. Her blue eyes, set far apart, gave an impression of candor, yet it was the square clean cut chin, which

while preventing her from being beautiful, stamped
her character as forceful.

Possibly Mona's aunt, Ella Singlefoot—arguably the most
memorable character in *Death Sails the Nile* with her caustic ob-
servations on the other female passengers on board the *Assuit*
("Long years of spinsterhood in a small southern town had made
her critical of women surrounded by male admirers. She had seized
upon each morsel of gossip concerning Celia Lawton . . . and had
devoured it avidly.")—was inspired by Frances' only real-life aunt,
Ida Frances Burks, the wife of beloved small-town doctor William
Martin Breeding, whom Frances would have known when she re-
sided in Livingston. Certainly Jimmie Bean, afflicted on the cruise
"with the boredom of one just out of college," recalls Frances'
brother, James Willis Burks III, who seems to have been something of a gay blade in the 'Thirties, attracted to women rather like
the former Follies dancer Sophie Worth.

As for the question of whether Agatha Christie might have been influenced by Frances Burks' Nile murder mystery, who really knows? The novel does not appear to have been published in England, but certainly its second murder—the stabbing of the blackmailing crewman Abdu, who is found clutching a fragment of a banknote in his hand—recalls the second murder in *Death in the Nile*, a novel which enjoys, if that is the right word, a similarly high body count. Additionally, the first murder victim, the wealthy, beautiful and proud American Celia Lawton, bears a certain resemblance to Christie's murdered American heiress, Linnet Doyle.

Although no *Death on the Nile*, to be sure, *Death Sails the Nile* in the estimation of contemporary critics was a fine detective novel, despite some technical blemishes characteristic of a novice in the field (see Chad Arment's afterword). In addition to the aforementioned praise for the book in the *Saturday Review*, *Death Sails the Nile* was lauded in the New York press by crime writer Norman Klein in the *New York Evening Post* ("Contains many an attack of gooseflesh—suspense very well maintained"), Isaac Anderson in the *New York Times Book Review* ("An exciting crime puzzle"), Will Cuppy in the *New York Herald Tribune* ("Has real excitement, not to mention an interesting background, shuddery until the final revelation"). The American heartland chimed in with praise as well, the *Minneapolis Star*, for example, assuring readers, "You'll find clues aplenty and a logical plot, but [as well] some queer turns that will surprise you. . . . [The author] has indeed made an auspicious start."[5]

With such reviews as these, Frances Burks seemingly had ample reason to launch Mona Case on a second amateur mystery investigation, yet soon after the publication of her book she seems effectively to have laid down her pen. Although Frances had hopefully dedicated *Death Sails the Nile* to her husband Silas, her character Ella Singlefoot's rueful reflection on men and marriage—"So much was demanded of their wives, yet the men themselves were frequently indiscreet"—hints at the draining emotional storms that lay ahead of the couple. It is most regrettable that intense marital turmoil capsized Frances Burks' nascent mystery writing career, but happily her sole detective novel, a worthy example of Golden

Age art and artifice, now stands as a tribute, in its own modest way, to a woman of evident promise.

ENDNOTES

[1] However, Agatha Christie may get the last laugh yet again, for the same year, 1933, in which *Death Sails the Nile* appeared, saw the publication by Christie of a Parker Pyne mystery short story entitled—you guessed it—"Death on the Nile." Of course the Western world at this time was especially fascinated with ancient Egypt as a result of the discovery, eleven years earlier, of Pharaoh Tutankhamen's marvelous lost tomb. Christie herself had opportunistically published an Hercule Poirot mystery short story, "The Adventure of the Egyptian Tomb," in September 1923, less than a year after the opening of tomb of "King Tut," as he had been colloquially dubbed.

[2] In modern value James Atkins' real and personal estate was worth over a million dollars in 1860, though the wealth he amassed was widely distributed at his death among no less than fourteen children. On the Lation Scott lynching see Margaret Vandiver's *Lethal Punishment: Lynchings and Legal Executions in the South* (Rutgers University Press, 2006) and the key contemporary account, "The Burning at Dyersburg: An NAACP Investigation," *The Crisis* 16 (February 1918):178-183.

[3] See Linda Jones Hall, "Clyde Pharr, the Women of Vanderbilt, and the Wyoming Judge: The Story behind the Translation of the Theodosian Code in Mid-Century America," *Roman Legal Tradition* 8 (2012), 24-25. Hall reports that at the time Frances Burks attended Vanderbilt women "dominated graduate studies in the Department of Classics" (p. 13).

4 Perhaps the best-known book published by The Stratford Press is civil rights activist and author WEB DuBois' *The Gift of Black Folk: The Negroes in the Making of America* (1924). It was published as part of the Knights of Columbus Racial Contribution Series, which also included George Cohen's *The Jews in the Making of America* (1924), also published by The Stratford Company. This was a daring project in the decade that saw the mass revival in America of the Ku Klux Klan and a successful effort to curtail the immigration of ethnicities and races which were then deemed undesirable. The Stratford Company also published Silas Bent McKinley's first book, *Democracy and Military Power* (1934), which included a foreword by famed progressive historian Charles Beard.

5 Interestingly, from the *Star* in the same number came a negative review to *The Bowstring Murders*, a novel by acknowledged genre master John Dickson Carr: "Mix a peculiar household with a half-insane English peer, a murder without clues and a detective who can work only when he has paid tribute to Bacchus, and you have 'The Bowstring Murders' . . . It's all very mysterious, and just as much of a mystery is the problem of why publishers can't decide that readers would like something plausible once in a while." Even genre masters have occasional misses!

DEATH SAILS
THE NILE

CHAPTER I
NUSA TRADES IN DEATH

Deep tropical blackness enveloped a little steamer on the river Nile. Dim lights hanging at long intervals around the deck were inadequate to penetrate the gloom that was as smothering now as the hot glare of the sun had been at midday.

The boat was always tied to the shore shortly after dusk. Sand and mud banks in the river channel made navigation dangerous at night and no river captain would sail after sundown, except in an emergency, for fear of being hopelessly grounded.

Despite the darkness two passengers were braving the evening's chill peculiar to upper Africa. They were Mona Case and Jimmie Bean, standing by the rail in the shadows of the top deck.

Twenty-five years of active and strenuous American life had given Mona Case unusual poise and an air of assurance. In four years after leaving college she had established a definite place for herself in the newspaper world. But there had been no time for relaxation or travel. Suddenly the death of an uncle had made it possible for her to realize her travel ambition, and three months in foreign countries had not dulled her enthusiasm. She was as eager now to see strange lands and people as the day she sailed from New York.

She was of medium height, slender, with a mass of short auburn curls topping a well-shaped head. She combined in her person the qualities of physical strength and vivacious charm. Her blue eyes, set far apart, gave an impression of candor, yet it was the square clean-cut chin, which while preventing her from being beautiful, stamped her character as forceful.

But if Mona were eager and enthusiastic, such was not the case with the tall young man who stood beside her on the deck.

"I can see by the way it starts out," said Jimmie Bean, with the boredom of one just out of college, "that this is going to be a hell of a trip. The food is terrible, and what a crowd. These people are too high-hat for me. I'm used to traveling Tourist Third, where something happens all the time."

"It's thrilling enough—the thought of sailing into the interior of Africa! I admit the afternoon was beastly hot."

"Yes and the Captain says each day will be hotter."

"Well, my Aunt Ella created a lot of excitement today when she lost her handbag. Did you hear about it?"

"No. How'd she lose it?"

"As a matter of fact, she didn't really lose it. She thought she did. About the time she was ready to leave the hotel for the steamer she discovered one of her bags, a small blue overnight case, was missing. She had the hotel manager, the room clerk and even the native servants hunting for it but they couldn't find it. Finally she gave up and rushed down to the boat just before sailing time."

"But I thought you said she didn't really lose it."

"That's the queer part about the whole thing. When we walked into her cabin there stood the blue case along with the rest of her baggage."

"Hm! Was anything stolen out of it?"

"Nothing was missing except a large celluloid soap box which Aunt Ella insists she put in the bag. That seems a silly thing to steal, especially when there was some jewelry and traveler's cheques in the side pocket. However, it must have been stolen because we found a piece of wet soap lying loose in the bag and Aunt Ella would never have done a thing like that. She's a very meticulous packer."

"A soap box! Well, I'll be darned! Who do you suppose would take a soap box? Certainly not a native. They aren't bothered with cleanliness, or godliness either, for that matter."

They lapsed into silence for a moment and then Jimmie spoke suddenly, pointing to a light that gleamed and twinkled on the still, black shore.

"Looks like someone lives there. I wonder who it is. I don't see another light anywhere and the Captain said we wouldn't reach a village until tomorrow."

"Why not ask the steward?" suggested Mona. "He's collecting our coffee cups on the other side of the deck."

Jimmie left her and walked across to the big-lipped Arab who was busy clearing a small table beside a potted plant. He did not seem to understand the boy's question at first and kept shaking his head negatively.

Then a wise look displaced the blankness in his opaque eyes.

"That belongs to sheik—Nusa. Great man, Nusa. Very good snake charmer."

Jimmie's face was avid with interest. "I wish he'd come down to the boat."

The Arab smiled a superior smile.

"He no come to boat ever. You go to him? He has many snakes."

"Not a bad idea. How far is it?"

"Quick walk." He looked at Jimmie's tall, thin figure and then at Mona's outlined slimly against the dark palm trees on the bank. "Pretty soon if long legs go alone, not so soon with lady."

"Can we go ashore? I mean, is the gangplank down?"

"Against orders for gangplank," said the Arab flatly. He looked over his shoulder and then added in a voice tinged with slyness. "Boat close to tree root. Easy to step over."

"Would it be safe for a lady to visit Nusa?"

"Plenty safe."

Jimmie pressed five piasters into the rough, thin fingers and returned to Mona.

"I've always wanted to see a snake charmer," she said. "Do you think a man can actually charm a snake?"

"Let's go." Jimmie took her arm and silently they climbed off the ship into the darkness. A little path led through drooping palm trees toward the twinkling light.

"I wish we'd brought a flash-light," grumbled Mona as she stumbled over a tree root. "It wouldn't be so funny if we stepped on a stray viper."

"Oh, Nusa has 'em all charmed," reassured Jimmie airily, though he himself was casting apprehensive glances into the shadowy foliage. It was damned silly of them not to have brought a torch. He had a few matches in his pocket but decided to save them until later.

They reached the end of the narrow little lane. Jimmie then struck a match and held it up to see a low, mud-brick structure with but one window from which came the light.

"There doesn't seem to be any door," he said in surprise.

"Maybe it's on the other side."

They felt their way around the corner of the dark, squatty house. Jimmie lit another of his precious matches.

"I see an opening," whispered Mona pointing to a dirty yellow curtain that served as a door.

"Do you suppose we ought to go in?" Jimmie was frankly dubious.

Mona hesitated only for the space of a second.

"Of course. Even if Nusa wanted to he wouldn't dare harm us. All natives are scared to death of the English government. By the way, have you any money with you?"

Jimmie patted his pocket. "Something more than a pound. He ought to be willing to show us all the snakes in Egypt for less than that."

"Let's knock."

Jimmie complied and rapped on the frame of the opening.

There was no response, only the sound of their breathing as they stood waiting in the dark. He knocked again with the same result.

Mona turned to Jimmie and said, impatiently, "Why don't we go on in? Probably a hallway is just inside with the main door leading off from it. Maybe we'll get more response if we knock on that."

The thought of going into this strange house, unannounced and uninvited, did not appeal to Jimmie but his masculine pride would not allow him to admit it.

"I'll go first," he offered with very little enthusiasm in his voice and striking a match, pushed aside the curtain.

They found themselves in what appeared to be a small square ante-chamber. Jimmie's match burnt his fingers. Dropping it with an exclamation he started to light another, when there came the sound of a door creaking on its hinges. A pale light penetrated the room and the two looked up to see a woman clothed in black standing in the doorway at the top of three rickety steps. She wore a Mohammedan veil pulled across her face, the only uncovered part of her body being a slender brown hand which rested on the knob of the door. She was like some dark specter appearing on the horizon of the unknown.

Mona was the first to recover from their surprise, caused by the sudden appearance of the native woman.

"Nusa," she pronounced the two syllables very distinctly. "We want to see Nusa."

The shrouded figure without a word closed the door and left them in pitch darkness.

"This room is like a tomb," muttered Jimmie, and Mona agreed.

"Good place for pack rats," she said, cold shivers racing up her spine at the thought. Her enthusiasm had waned perceptibly.

The door opened again and they were ushered into a long narrow windowless compartment, hung with bright colored cloths, its floor covered with matting. The only light came from a brazier hung on a chain from the ceiling. There were divans all the way around the walls. A large brass tray resting on a Mashribia stand held two empty coffee cups and a half-eaten plate of dates. Had Nusa been entertaining another nocturnal visitor?

"Wonder if the old bird will see us?" whispered Jimmie as he lighted a cigarette.

The room seemed to Mona to lull away all thoughts of danger. It was sensuous in its calmative effect. She wondered who Nusa's visitor could be. Perhaps a sheik of the desert or a relative from down the Nile. Certainly someone had been burning incense recently in the room, for the air was heavy with an odor entirely strange to her occidental nose. Mona's imagination carried her back to the Pharaohs who ruled along the banks of the Nile, and to the time when Caesar and Anthony wooed Cleopatra. She wondered what kind of snake really killed the Egyptian Queen and if Nusa could have charmed such a snake. Perhaps there were still vipers like it. She thought how exciting it would be to see one. She planned to ask Nusa if it were possible.

A door must have swung open somewhere in the house, for a slight draft caused the light in the brazier to flicker and a sound of voices came from beyond the far corner of the room. Someone was speaking French in a high nervous tone. Mona became rigid with attention. The words that stimulated her drowsy senses like an electric shock were, "So you desire, for your own use, two deadly vipers." Mona looked at Jimmie to see if he had heard this startling statement and then remembered he did not understand French. She leaned forward herself to listen, her pulse racing wildly, her heart thumping loudly.

She could hear only one side of the conversation. Nusa's visitor spoke too low for her to catch a single word.

The snake charmer himself continued at intervals in the cracked voice of an old man.

"I do you this favor since you come as the friend of my friend. He did for me once a favor. I am a humble follower of Mohammed. I return that favor. I am true son of Allah and remember well the words of the most high prophet, 'An eye for an eye, and a tooth for a tooth.'"

There was an answering murmur and then came the words that propelled Mona noiselessly to the corner of the room.

"In this tiny box are two asps rich with venom. Take care they do not sting you, for certain death awaits the careless one."

Softly pulling aside a heavy curtain she found the door which apparently had swung slightly open a few minutes before, allowing her to overhear the conversation. Jimmie, his mouth open with unvoiced surprise, followed her. They peered through the narrow opening and found themselves looking upon a most amazing scene. An old Arab with white turban, swarthy face and black beard, sat squatting on his heels before a large wicker basket. Beside a sputtering candle lay a gray ball of woolen thread and a pair of blackened tweezers. His visitor could not be seen, for he was hidden from sight by the door which Mona dared not open further. The basket itself was the focal point, for it was quivering as if from a living, throbbing force within. With a quick gesture of his brown, bony hand Nusa removed the wicker top and disclosed a writhing mass of hooded cobras. He was crooning softly to the serpents, whose heads with hoods outspread were even now waving above the top of the basket. The weird moaning by the charmer, combined with the threshing of the snakes' bodies against the woven grass sides, gave forth an incantatory sound as eerie as it was diabolical.

Suddenly hearing a noise from behind, the two turned to find the menacing figure of the woman in black standing at their very elbows. Overcome with horror at the scene and feeling the guiltiness of one caught spying upon secrets, Mona grabbed Jimmie's arm and, without a word of explanation, literally pulled him through the silent house and out into the night.

"What in the world is the matter?" gasped Jimmie as he ran after her down the shadowy path.

She gave him no answer until they were safely aboard the boat and then she repeated the conversation she had overheard.

"What do you suppose anybody would want with a couple of death adders?" It was Jimmie's turn to be excited. "I wish we could have seen what Nusa's visitor looked like."

"I'm going to my cabin," said Mona abruptly. "I'm tired of this awful darkness."

They left the gloom of the dimly lighted deck. Their haste to go below was unfortunate, for if they had waited a few minutes Jimmie would have gotten his wish, since out of the deep shade of the palm trees came a heavily cloaked figure bearing a small but terrible burden. It was Nusa's nocturnal visitor stealthily returning to the defenseless little boat.

CHAPTER II
NINE ON THE NILE

Three days had elapsed since the *Assuit* had started on its hazardous trip up the Nile to Wadi Halfa. Hazardous because it was the middle of March and the river was very low. There would be difficulty in getting the boat through. The Sudanese sailors were already grumbling about it. They hated to pole in the growing heat.

Dr. Bradshaw, who served in the capacity of captain and doctor on the *dahabeah*, was having trouble with them. He himself disliked making the trip when the water had receded, but what could he do about it? Nine perfectly good paying passengers wanted to visit the ancient temple of Abu Simbel and the African Marine Company in this bad season was only too glad to run a boat for them. Little the company cared if the sailors poled or the Captain sweated. It had sold expensive tickets in a dull season. Let the boat get through as best it could.

Nine passengers! Mona sitting alone in the smoking salon thought about the other eight as she balanced the after-dinner coffee cup on her knee and lighted a cigarette. They were all so different. Not different in a pleasant spicy way, as are Egyptian cigarettes, but different in a harsh, disagreeable contrast. Perhaps this realization was driven home so emphatically because of the enforced contiguity. Nine people of varied tastes were cooped up together on a small, creaking boat, the Captain was dour and the servants and sailors obviously resentful beneath their deferential manner.

Yes, they were a varied lot. Take the archaeologist, Professor Cross, for instance. He was short, thin and ascetic looking. The queer little clucking sounds he made with his lips when he spoke,

33

combined with a shambling gait and a detached manner, labeled him as one who had spent his life in the assimilation of cold facts both in the schoolroom and on lonely archaeological expeditions. He was an authority on certain phases of Egyptology and had written several long, erudite volumes on the subject. From his bloodless, claw-like hands and his pale, expressionless eyes one got the impression that his learning was not of a vigorous, healthy species but of a dry, dusty, academic nature. He seldom spoke except to elucidate problems of antiquity and was by no means sociable in his contacts with the other passengers. Mona sensed the journalistic possibilities in this little man but at the same time realized the hopelessness of ever penetrating his reserve.

Jack Spencer, on the other hand, was as genial as the Professor was forbidding. In his late thirties, he was tall and slender with an indefinable air of distinction in the way he held his shoulders. His eyes were dark blue, his hair and mustache black, tinged with a little gray. He was obviously a man who had seen the world and enjoyed it. He radiated cordiality and charm just as naturally as Professor Cross bottled up every emotion within himself.

Mona's thoughts went to Celia Lawton—beautiful, exotic Celia, rumored engaged to one man in the party and pursued by two others. She was, by all odds, the central figure on the boat. Mona remembered the first time she had seen her, standing on the terrace of the Semiramis Hotel in Cairo. Celia had been dressed in a pale green clinging suit, her hat, with its jaunty feather, perched upon the back of her head allowing masses of ash blonde hair to show. Her eyes matched her clothes, for they were of the color of the sea in a frolicking mood. Then, as now, she was a magnet that attracted to its dynamic center every male eye within range, and every woman's, too, for that matter, though the one was filled with admiration and desire, while the other was torn between jealousy and curiosity. Celia herself was just as fascinatingly remote, just as charmingly impervious to it all, as might be some cool, beautiful star twinkling in the eastern sky, far removed from earthly hands though enticingly generous to their gaze. It was this aloofness, this far-away look in her eyes that held one's attention. Perhaps it was a note of sadness there, a note of longing yet unfulfilled that was so appealing. Each man's heart beat warmly in his breast to protect her, to give her that happiness which somehow one felt she needed.

Mona smiled down into her empty coffee cup. Perhaps by the end of their journey she would know this woman better. It was a pleasant thought. Pleasant in the irritation and general unrest that enveloped the hot little boat.

"Why the Cheshire grin?" Jimmie was peering in at her from the half-opened door.

Mona almost dropped her coffee cup at the sudden interruption to her thoughts. She stared at Jimmie as he slipped into a chair beside her.

"I was just thinking," she said.

"Well, if it was something agreeable, please tell me. This is the gloomiest tub I was ever on. No one's enjoying himself except Celia and Spencer and even they look fed up at times. Certainly the only excitement I've had was the other night when we visited the snake charmer and that wouldn't do as a steady diet. By the way, where were you at dinner? I admit it was the usual bum feed but still we've got to eat."

"Oh, I slept through the heat of the afternoon and didn't get my tea until five-thirty. It's simply a case of too many cakes and too many cups of white tea."

"Well, you missed something. That Worthington woman was up to her old tricks."

"Tricks? What do you mean?"

"Haven't you noticed her? She gets worse every day—flirting with Jack Spencer just as if she weren't married. I don't see why her husband puts up with her. As far as I can judge, he's rather a good sort."

"You must be exaggerating, Jimmie. Aunt Ella, who is quite a fan of Sophie's, claims she simply adores her husband."

"Maybe you're right, but just the same she was flirting with Jack at dinner."

"Granted she was, I don't think that's so bad. After all, why shouldn't she make eyes at Jack? Goodness knows, he's attractive enough. Besides, her husband trails around with Celia every chance he gets."

"She can enjoy her woman's rights just as long as she leaves me alone. I'm no grave-robber."

"I don't believe she's a day over thirty," defended Mona.

"Thirty nothing! She's forty and her hair's been blondeened so often that the tops of her ears are a pale yellow."

"And you try to tell me men are not cats," retorted Mona with heavy sarcasm.

"Here, here, what's the row about?" boomed a voice from behind their backs.

The two turned to find Tom Amory standing alone in the doorway. He was a broad-shouldered giant of a man with coal-black hair, beetling eyebrows and a sullen slant to his jaw. It was rumored that he was Celia's fiancé but whether this were true or not, no one knew.

Tom went on in his deep voice: "What are you two arguing about now?"

"We weren't arguing." Jimmie's tone was condescending. "Mona's wrong but I can't convince her. She thinks Sophie's thirty and I'd be willing to bet real money she's at least forty."

"Well now," said Tom, "you're both wrong." He stood before them, his hands rammed down into his pockets, his eyes thoughtful. "I happen to know how old she really is. Sophie and Celia went to school together and Celia says she's thirty-five. Sophie herself claims she's thirty. A little fibbing about her age won't hurt. Here she comes now."

Sophie's rather noisy laughter was heard in the corridor just outside the glass door. There was little humor in it and even less in Colonel Worthington's answering rumble.

She preceded him into the room and stood for a moment surveying the group. Undoubtedly she was attractive in a sensual way, with her baby-blue eyes, blonde hair and rounded curves, but there seemed to be a negative quality to her beauty. One had the impression that it was nature's desperate attempt to cover a mediocre mind busy with nonessentials. And yet Mona was not sure whether she thought her exceedingly clever or utterly stupid. Certainly she never made any remarks in public that indicated brilliance.

With his erect carriage and quick, springy step, Colonel Worthington was a typical British army officer. He was of medium height, a bit heavy but possessing the elasticity of movement acquired from a vigorous life in the open. His face was tanned by exposure to tropical suns, his mouth hard and grim from long years of command at isolated army posts in India. His hair was iron gray, while his close-clipped mustache remained dark. His manner was brusque, often to the point of rudeness.

With irritation written on his face he followed his wife into the room. He made no pretense of finding her a chair but, instead, settled himself in front of the oil grate and drew a meerschaum pipe from his pocket. An imperceptible nod was his only recognition of the others.

Jimmie stepped into the breach by offering Sophie his chair.

"You'll want to sit close to the fire, Mrs. Worthington," he said, avoiding Mona's eyes. "It's rather chilly in here tonight."

"Thank you." Sophie shivered as she sank into the wicker chair.

"One lump or two?" Tom waited for her answer, the sugar tongs poised in mid-air.

"One, if you please." She was strangely silent.

"We might as well make ourselves comfortable," said Tom, still standing, his back to the Colonel. "Professor Cross is lecturing this evening on the wonders of Abu Simbel, the temple we're going to see tomorrow, and once he gets started there'll be no stopping him. At that, I suppose the temple really is worth hearing about. It's probably the most wonderful of the whole lot."

Professor Cross followed by Miss Singlefoot, who now as always was close beside him, came into the room at this point in the conversation and Tom turned to him with the question, "Am I right in saying Abu Simbel is in a class by itself, Professor?"

"Quite right. In my estimation it is the most important of the remains of Nubian antiquity." The little man stood by the fire rubbing his hands, which looked as if they had never been warm. "If you like," he suggested timidly although his face was alight with interest, "after we have had our coffee, I will tell you a little about the temple and the tombs that surround it."

"Oh, that would be delightful," piped Miss Singlefoot. "You can make it a lot more interesting than a stupid guidebook."

Colonel Worthington removed his pipe long enough to inquire, "Hadn't we better wait for the others?"

"That's true," said Tom in a vain attempt to appear casual. "Celia isn't here."

"Nor Spencer," put in Miss Singlefoot meaningly.

Mona suddenly felt sorry for Tom. It was characteristic of Aunt Ella to be malicious where she thought a question of morals was concerned. Long years of spinsterhood in a small southern town had made her critical of women surrounded by male admirers. She had seized upon each morsel of gossip concerning Celia Lawton and Tom and had devoured it avidly. It pleased her to witness a rift between the two, for in her opinion only the most conventional love affair should progress unobstructed. Besides, of the two men she preferred Spencer. He had been a willing listener to her rambling account of how she and Mona had inherited John Singlefoot's estate and why she had come to Egypt. She had told him, her eyes owl-like, her thin, angular body hunched forward confidentially, that she didn't believe in young women traveling abroad unchaperoned. Spencer had solemnly agreed with these sentiments, thereby winning in Ella Singlefoot a staunch ally.

Ten minutes passed without the appearance of the absent members and by now everyone had finished his coffee.

"Why not start your talk, Professor Cross?" suggested Miss Singlefoot. "The others may not have any intention of coming. Anyway, we can't waste the evening waiting for them."

A general murmur of approval greeted this suggestion to which the Professor acquiesced with astonishing affability.

"The temple of Abu Simbel," he began in a high-pitched voice, "lies on the west bank of the Nile, and is one of the most awe-inspiring and artistic of Egyptian ruins. Hewn out of a sheer sandstone cliff, it was, in ancient times, the largest and most magnificent edifice in Nubia. The King of Kings, Rameses the Great, built it in commemoration of his conquests. Rameses II was in reality the greatest conqueror of antiquity, prior to the Roman and Grecian era, and to him we owe many of the wonderful temples on the Nile, and also many elaborate tombs, some of which we shall see tomorrow. In front of this particular temple to Abu Simbel, there are the magnificent colossi of King Rameses II and his wife, Queen Nofretere. The roof of the great hall is supported by eight square pillars dedicated to Osiris, the great Judge of the Underworld. At the extreme end of the temple is the Sanctuary, cut out of the rock. And that, not to go into too great detail, is the temple of Abu Simbel, who is known as the Father of the Ear of Corn."

"But what about the tombs?" asked Miss Singlefoot in a sudden rush of words. "If there are any interesting ones I do hope they're near the temple, for I don't intend to ride miles and miles on a rickety donkey again."

Professor Cross had become strangely amiable and reassuring. "Several very interesting tombs are close to the temple. They are burial places of various important leaders in Rameses II's campaigns. These men became rich and famous by their conquests and so their tombs were built not far from the great temple. The tomb that you must not fail to see is one of a wealthy official, Ameni Amenaret by name, of the reign of Rameses II. In a large inner room which is known as the funeral chamber, there is a hideous figure of the jackal-headed Anubis, God of the Underworld. This figure, cut out on the western wall, covers a false door representing the entrance to the Realm of the Dead."

"What's all this stuffy talk about the dead and tombs and temples?" Celia, radiant and very much alive, stood in the doorway. Her cheeks were pink from their contact with the cold air, her eyes shining, her smile mocking and elusive.

No one spoke for a second. Mona was surprised to see a steely glint come into the eyes of Professor Cross and then quickly disappear. She felt that she had seen behind a curtain which was seldom drawn.

Jack Spencer, after making sure that Celia was comfortably settled, now busied himself at the coffee table.

"It's remarkable," he said with a careless glance at Tom, "how many stars are out tonight. Celia and I were fascinated. This is the first evening they've been brilliant. We hated to come in even for our coffee."

"Not really," Tom was being very polite. "Wasn't it cold out there?"

Sophie's metallic laughter, breaking forth at this moment, sounded harsh and discordant. She and Miss Singlefoot had been whispering together.

"Really, my dear," said her husband, "I wish you wouldn't laugh that way. You make me nervous."

Sophie said nothing but stared at him with an inexplicable light in her eyes. Her lips moved but no sound came.

"We are all nervous," broke in Professor Cross, unexpectedly. "It's the long days of heat."

"Nervous, hell!" Tom spat the words contemptuously. "None of you know what it means to be nervous. Ask a man condemned to death; he knows."

"Would death be so bad?" murmured Celia, thoughtfully. "Somehow I don't feel that way about it."

"Speaking of death," remarked Jimmie, taking deep puffs on his cigarette, "do you know what the name of this tub, *Assuit*, means?"

"The City of the Dead," clucked Professor Cross' thin lips. "Assuit is an ancient Egyptian word meaning 'village or home of those who have departed this life.' There is a town of that name situated on the Nile. You passed it coming from Cairo to Luxor."

"City of the Dead, indeed," quavered Miss Singlefoot. "I'd just as soon this boat had another name. I don't mind visiting gloomy places, but I can't say I like to live in them."

"I wonder where Dr. Bradshaw is tonight," said Jack Spencer suddenly and irrelevantly. "He's generally on hand for his coffee."

"He's in the stern talking to the sailors. They've been complaining a lot today. They blame him every time we hit a mud bank." Celia smiled at Tom as she spoke.

"You seem to know a lot about it." He did not return the smile. She lapsed into silence, a troubled look clouding her eyes.

"For crying out loud, what's wrong with everybody?" asked Jimmie. "We'll be murdering each other in our beds tonight at this rate."

"Well, I'm sure no one would accuse me of being cross," remarked Miss Singlefoot rather acidly. "Anyway, everything was perfectly agreeable until a little while ago. We were learning so much from the Professor."

Colonel Worthington knocked his pipe loudly against the side of the stove. "I think I'll be turning in," he said. "We have a hard day before us tomorrow and I must do a few things before I go to bed."

He rose and nodded to his wife.

"How about you, dear?"

"I'm ready." Her voice was flat, expressionless.

The others stood up almost with one accord.

"Tomorrow will be a big day," said Spencer. "We've had three nasty hot ones but I think the temple and tombs will be worth our efforts. Don't forget, Celia, to get the pair of smoked glasses from Mona." He suppressed a yawn with difficulty.

"Thank you, Jack, for reminding me." Celia turned to Mona with one of her irresistible smiles. "May I come by for them now?"

"Do," said Mona cordially. "You'll need them—the glare of the sun is terrific."

"I shan't mind it," answered Celia. "I'll be only too glad to get off this boat. It's so hot and so dull here doing nothing. Thank goodness, tomorrow something will happen."

And it did.

CHAPTER III
BEFORE ANUBIS, GOD OF THE DEAD

One hour after sunrise the passengers disembarked on the sandy Nubian shore. They were a sleepy, somewhat incongruously clad crowd, wearing light top coats as protection against the penetrating chill of the early morning hours and sun helmets in anticipation of the midday heat. They had time for little more than a fleeting glance at Abu Simbel lying in the distance, cool and serene, before they were surrounded by dark-skinned boys loudly proclaiming the merits of their respective beasts of burden. Natives and donkeys milled about them in an ever-thickening circle of dust until they were mounted and ready to start off across the desert to the tombs.

Miss Singlefoot had picked out a raw-boned nag chiefly because its coat was cut into intricate and even artistic Egyptian designs. On this small African burro she looked suspiciously like a caricature of Don Quixote. Her long legs dangled a few inches above the ground and her loosely-constructed frame teetered uncertainly in the saddle. She was galloping along at a rapid pace, her veil flying in the breeze, her skirt flapping against the sides of the donkey, when she realized suddenly that the animal's head-long speed was carrying her far in advance of the rest of the party. Frantically but unsuccessfully she pulled upon the rope reins. Then with the little wind she had left she called imploringly to the donkey boy who was running along behind her, nonchalantly beating the animal's hind-quarters with a large stick.

Mona, convulsed with laughter, finally caught up with her aunt. By this time the Arab boy had swung onto the donkey's tail and slowed him down.

"I declare, Mona," panted Miss Singlefoot, "one more minute on this wild beast and I would have been killed." Turning to the boy she vented her wrath upon him.

"Look here, you limb of Satan. Haven't you any sense at all? Mind you now, make this mule go slower!"

In response he grinned widely and came back at her with the inevitable sing-song refrain, "Nice donkey, lady, good donkey! Everything all right?"

"Humph," snorted Miss Singlefoot, "you are all ignoramuses, the whole lot of you! But go slow from now on—slow I say!" She screamed it quite as if she expected him to understand her English if it were loud enough.

"I'll ride along with you, Aunt Ella," said Mona, "and we'll take it easy from now on."

Miss Singlefoot looked back to see if Professor Cross were close behind, but he was in the distance jogging along beside Sophie who appeared to be having trouble with her donkey.

Celia, as usual, was leading a train composed of Spencer and Colonel Worthington, Jimmie and Tom being a little in the rear of them.

Ten minutes later they reached a low sandstone ridge whose sides were dotted with dark holes indicating the tombs behind them. It was the third tomb to which they made their way, and at its entrance all dismounted, Miss Singlefoot heaving a loud sigh of relief and muttering under her breath unmentionable and unladylike threats at all donkey boys.

On entering the tomb they passed through a low-vaulted passageway, its walls covered with the figures of Osiris, Judge of the Underworld, and Anubis, King of the Dead. The passage led to a gloomy little room about ten feet square.

"Phew," gasped Miss Singlefoot, "this is a clammy spot. I don't doubt it was a tomb. How do we get out of here?"

Professor Cross looked at her with his pale, cold eyes.

"You are not ready to go out," he said.

"It gives me the creeps, too," put in Sophie. "You don't mean we go down these dark steps, do you?"

She pointed to some steep steps that led only into a pool of darkness.

"Dr. Bradshaw," said Professor Cross, his voice sounding hollow in the vaulted chamber, "we have some lights, haven't we?"

"Certainly," replied the doctor, and took from his pocket a bunch of candles. "They've never put electricity in this tomb."

"I think I'll wait up here while you go down," quavered Miss Singlefoot nervously. "I never liked dark steps."

She looked gaunt in the half light.

"I'll stay with you," offered Sophie.

"Don't be silly," remarked her husband irritably. "You and Miss Singlefoot don't want to stay here with just him." He pointed to a tall, powerful-looking black man who had let them into the tomb.

Miss Singlefoot glanced timorously at the native who seemed to leer at her out of the dusk.

"I'm going down," she said, desperation in her voice.

With the light from the flickering candles throwing grotesque shadows upon the wall the little group slowly descended. The steps turned sharply at the bottom and stopped abruptly in a narrow black passage.

"These walls are very interesting," began Professor Cross. "It is through here that the ancients brought their corpses to the mortuary chapel beyond!"

His high-pitched voice reminded Mona of a priest's chant in the still, dead air.

"It is too close in here for me," murmured Celia and left Professor Cross' monotonous discourse to wander on into the next room which in ancient times had been used as a funeral hall. The walls were covered around the top and bottom with figures of Anubis, some large, some small, but all wearing that awe-inspiring head of the jackal. The huge black figure on the west wall attracted Celia's attention immediately.

She stood before it, holding her candle aloft. In the wavering light the terrible face of the God seemed to be alive. Its stern lips were half opened as if ready to pronounce a last judgment.

Celia shuddered and felt suddenly cold. She rammed her left hand down into her pocket. For a moment her whole body stiffened, then with a fearful scream she fell to the floor, her arms outflung. Not a sound followed but the echoing of that scream and the dull thud of her body striking the lifeless sand.

CHAPTER IV
THE MARK OF THE SNAKE

Celia was dead. Twenty minutes after she fell upon the sand in that vault of death all life had left her body. And with its going fled the secret of her agonizing scream.

Dr. Bradshaw had been unable to do anything for her. She was completely paralyzed until death. By the time the Arab runner had brought the doctor's medicine kit from the boat there was no need for it.

What killed her? No one knew. Or if any one did, he gave no sign.

Dr. Bradshaw would not make a statement. From the hasty examination in the tomb he had gotten nothing. Very little anyhow. The body had begun to grow cold almost before the heart action stopped. It was stiff when he first lifted it from the floor. The hands were clenched in two little fists, the eyes stared up in heart-breaking anguish.

There was something terrifying about those eyes. They were like eyes of an animal blinded with pain, yet they were the only part of Celia that showed a spark of life. They seemed to be trying to speak above all their suffering. What was the message they struggled to convey? Was it a warning?

Dr. Bradshaw was troubled. He sat at his desk, his eyes staring through the porthole that presented a series of desolate panoramas. But he didn't see them—his thoughts were all grappling with the problem at hand. It was gloomy enough. Celia Lawton was dead and he was not able to say why. She had been a passenger on the boat on which he was Ship Doctor, as well as Captain. He was responsible and an unsatisfactory death certificate would not be accepted by the African Marine Company. She had died, and there was a reason back of it all.

He shook his head mournfully. He had other worries. Going downstream, the boat was two days from a telephone or telegraph. The weather was very hot. It was unthinkable to bury the body in a tomb like the one in which she had died.

It must be gotten back to Assuan. But would the sailors stand for it? They were ignorant, superstitious and shunned all contact with the dead even though their proximity to it consisted merely in being on the same boat. Moreover, they would want to know what caused her death and if they received no answer would suspect the worst. And what was the worst? That she had been murdered!

Dr. Bradshaw turned a stubby pencil nervously between his fingers. All this thinking just made it more difficult. But he must think. If she had been murdered that meant a murderer was aboard the boat. And other mysterious deaths might follow.

He flung the pencil from him and rose to his feet. Damn! Why did this terrible thing have to happen? He paced the floor. Perhaps there was a normal explanation for her death—maybe angina pectoris or a stroke of paralysis due to high blood pressure. But no, she was too young. Just past thirty and apparently healthy. A mere slip of a woman. Scarcely five feet tall.

Dr. Bradshaw stopped dead still. A mere slip of a woman. Outflung arms. Clenched fists. Paralysis. A quick death.

He stared above him at his book shelf. Yes, it was there, the book he wanted. He found the page. "Two little marks," it read, "two little marks close together and scarcely visible in the flesh." He slapped the book shut and started from the room.

No one was in the corridor. He unlocked Celia Lawton's door and went in, carefully fastening it behind him.

The body was laid out on a small brass bed with strangely big knobs. The form looked so tiny under its white shroud—scarcely more than a child's.

Dr. Bradshaw pulled down the sheet. He put his hand under the head and gently lifted the body. Yes, it was light, very light. It must have weighed little more than ninety pounds. The bones were so small.

He felt of the cheek. It startled him by its coldness. Something cold in a hot room. He shuddered. Could they get the body through this heat before—? He refused to go on.

Both fists were closed tightly. The fingers would have to be pried open. It would be difficult not to bruise them. He didn't like the idea. But then, did it matter? Bruised or unbruised, they would soon be dust.

He mustn't allow himself to become morbid. That was not a good way to begin. After all, he was a doctor. Doctors couldn't afford to be chicken-hearted.

He pried loose the cold, stiff fingers and opened the right hand. It looked pitifully small. How hard she had clenched it. The nails of her four fingers had bored deep under the skin. What agony she must have suffered! There were no other marks on her palm.

The left hand was harder to open. It seemed to be a little larger than the right. Funny. You'd think it would be smaller. The doctor didn't want to bruise the flesh. He stopped for a moment to mop his dripping forehead. Dashed hot business. Bad business—for any kind of weather.

He broke the grip. No wonder the hand seemed bigger. Why hadn't he noticed it? Not so keen as he used to be. The heat and endless stretches of sand had done that for him. The fingers were swollen. The whole inside of the hand was swollen. It was discolored, too. Terribly so. He lifted the wrist and with his eye measured the thickness of the palm. He compared it with the right. Twice as thick. What a fool he'd been.

Where was it thickest? He examined the hand carefully. Exactly in the center of the palm triangle. He wished for his microscope.

He shrugged his shoulders. It didn't matter. If the bed were pulled a little closer to the light that would do as well. The body seemed to move with the bed's motion. Damn his imagination. He must pull himself together. Just a little longer and it would be clear. Perhaps.

The light was much better. He flattened out the palm and held it up to the window. A queer, crooked smile of elation hovered around his lips for a second, then vanished. Two little marks close together and scarcely visible in the swollen flesh. There they were.

The doctor let the hand slip from his fingers. Celia Lawton had been bitten by a horned asp, the deadliest of vipers. But how? Serpents don't live in dry, dusty tombs. Besides she was not touching any wall when she fell. She had merely thrust her hand into her pocket. He had seen her. Perhaps, beneath that grim old god Anubis was a hiding place for vipers—vipers that lurked there through the ages, patient with their poison. Perhaps the greedy God of Death had grown lonesome without a victim. Perhaps, the curse of three thousand years ago was still alive and vicious. Perhaps—but no, it was all too fantastic, too repellent. He closed his eyes to put away the thought.

Another took its place, just as hideous. Someone must have put the asp in Miss Lawton's pocket. Among the passengers was a murderer. They couldn't leave him behind as they had left the black figure. There was a good reason. They didn't know who he was.

CHAPTER V
THE MURDERER CANNOT ESCAPE

Mona Case sat in her deck chair idly watching the unchanging out-line of the far distant sand hills—monotonous and deadly outposts of endless sand dunes. The boat was moving slowly ahead. The paddle wheel restlessly churning the dull, dirty water. Why were they not turning back? Celia couldn't be buried in that bleak, desolate country. It would be so lonesome there. But no, she couldn't be lonesome. She was dead and the dead are not anything.

Yet she was alive yesterday at this time. Alive and beautiful. Now she was dead and ugly. What was it that made her ugly? It must have been that look of horror in her eyes. Horror of what? Death. But she had said last night that she was not afraid of death.

Why had she died? If only it had been Sophie instead. Sophie who was so healthy. Somehow, Mona didn't like Sophie. She was loud and boisterous one minute, sullen and repressed the next.

But Celia hadn't been sickly looking. Only yesterday she had said she was never ill. And today she was dead.

Wasn't that Dr. Bradshaw coming up the steps? It was. He looked tired. His shoulders drooped wearily into his arms. Long arms for so short a man.

"Dr. Bradshaw," she called, as he halted at the top of the steps, his cheeks red, his rotund body quivering from the heat.

He did not answer but stood staring at her through thick-lensed glasses. He looked like a man who had seen a ghost. Mona felt suddenly chilled. There it was again—that queer sensation of evil which kept haunting her. Stolen bags, missing soap boxes, cold eyes reflecting colder souls, sudden death in a ghastly tomb.

"Dr. Bradshaw," she repeated, weakly determined to lay the ghost. "May I ask you a question?"

"What is it, Miss Case?" He had not heard her the first time. Probably he was just now seeing her. Before he had looked beyond into the hot deadly jungles of Africa.

"What caused Miss Lawton's death?" She wanted to say more. She wanted to say that it was such a shock to her—that she admired Celia so much—that Celia had given her the impression of never being ill. But she couldn't. Her tongue was cold against the roof of her mouth. Her lips moved mechanically.

The doctor spoke in a dull thick voice.

"Miss Lawton was murdered."

"I was afraid of that," said Mona.

"Why?" The question was like a rifle shot in thick, heavy atmosphere.

"Since that first day when Aunt Ella lost her bag I have felt something was going to happen. Just why, I don't know. A woman's intuition, perhaps." She hesitated for the briefest moment. "What caused her death?"

"She died of an asp bite. Asps don't live in dry, dusty caverns that are closed from light and air. They live in the hot sand."

"And she died in a cold tomb."

"Yes, that was unfortunate—unfortunate for the murderer."

Mona thought of the first night aboard when she and Jimmie had visited the snake charmer. The other nocturnal visitor must have been the murderer and she had no idea of his identity. She started to tell the doctor of the episode and then for no good reason changed her mind. Instead she asked him a question.

"What are you going to do about the murder?"

"Do about it? What can I do? Nothing!"

"But you must."

"I am merely a doctor, not a detective. Beyond my stethoscope I know very little. I am not clever enough." He smiled bitterly. "Besides, the murderer cannot escape. There are nothing but deserts on either side of the Nile. He couldn't live two days on those hot sands without provisions. At Assuan the police will take charge. It is their job."

"But meanwhile—?"

"I do not understand," he said.

"Don't you see?" she persisted. "There may be other murders."

"How can I stop them?" he asked helplessly.

"Perhaps we can't really stop them, but we can try."

"We?"

"Yes, I am going to help you. I am the logical one. You didn't murder her, neither did I. We can't trust the others."

"But you are so young. What do you know about murder?"

"I've read a great deal and my years of experience as a newspaper reporter will help. I have been assigned to cover many a murder trial and I've followed the evidence of most of the famous ones in the last four years."

Dr. Bradshaw shook his head wearily. He was evidently unconvinced.

"Meddling in this affair any further than is absolutely necessary is dangerous."

"Not meddling may be more dangerous," returned Mona. "At least, we have one thing to be thankful for. The murderer is tied to the boat. The treacherous river and these desolate sands will see to that. He cannot escape."

"Neither can his victim," said Dr. Bradshaw.

CHAPTER VI
QUESTIONS

The eight passengers on the *dahabeah* were congregated in the smoking lounge. They had been asked to come there by Dr. Bradshaw. No one knew why. That is, no one but Mona and, of course, the murderer.

An atmosphere of irritated suspense pervaded the room. Mona felt it tingling in her finger tips, pounding in her ears! Again a question she couldn't answer. Which one of the other seven was it?

Colonel Worthington and Sophie sat close together on the divan, each busy with his own gloomy thoughts; Miss Singlefoot talked in a high-pitched voice to Professor Cross who had a distracted air; Tom sat alone at one of the tea tables, nervously drumming his fingers on its polished top while Spencer, looking almost unperturbed, picked out chords on the piano. Jimmie stood staring out of the window, his long, slim fingers playing idly with the cord on the dingy shade.

"What I can't see," said Miss Singlefoot for the third time in the past ten minutes, "is why we're going on ahead as if nothing had happened. Wadi Halfa is certainly no place to take a dead—, er, I mean one who is deceased. I think we ought to be going back to Assuan or Cairo as fast as possible. It's absolutely indecent, this riding about for pleasure, when that poor thing lies in her room stiff and cold."

"No doubt Dr. Bradshaw has some reason for it." Spencer swung around on the piano stool. "And from now on pleasure is definitely out of the picture. For me, anyway."

"Maybe he's going to suggest that the funeral be up here in this God-forsaken hole. There's probably some fool law about burying the body immediately after death. But I won't stand for it. Law or no law, her body is going to be shipped home." Tom looked around the group belligerently, almost as if he expected one of them to disagree with him.

"Of course, of course," snapped Professor Cross. "No funeral will be held here. This is no fitting burial place. Nothing but ancient tombs."

"I never want to see another tomb," said Sophie in a shrill voice. "I can see Celia now lying in the dust before that awful God of Death. Oh, it was horrible."

"Let's not talk about it," murmured Spencer. "Here comes the doctor anyway."

As he spoke, Dr. Bradshaw's short, quick steps were heard in the corridor. He came in hurriedly, his prominent eyes passing lightly over the group.

"I am sorry to have kept you waiting so long," he said in an apologetic tone, "but the truth is I've been having a little trouble with the Arab sailors. The first mate came to me just now with the tale that they'd all quit if we didn't get rid of the corpse. He said it wasn't safe for the remaining passengers and the sailors to go ahead unless the body was buried. They are a very superstitious, fanatical lot and I thought for a moment the whole crew would strike in spite of all I could do. The first mate finally saw it my way and helped persuade the others to stick. I left them muttering something about the evil spirit getting us. However, I believe it will blow over by night."

"But, Dr. Bradshaw," interposed Colonel Worthington, "don't you really think we ought to be going back to Assuan instead of on to Wadi Halfa? We must get the body to an undertaker as soon as possible. This hot weather we are sailing in is bound to have its bad results. I can't understand why we haven't turned back before now." His manner was irritatingly polite.

"That is the first announcement I have to make to you," said the doctor, in a level tone. "In an hour we shall be at Adindan where we take on a fresh supply of vegetables and meat. Immediately after they are on board we will turn about and head for Assuan at full speed. With good weather and no bad luck we will be back at the first cataract within forty-five hours. I am sorry for this delay in getting started but I think you'll all prefer it to doing without food for two days and nights."

He stopped for a moment to glance at Mona. The look of encouragement on her face reassured him.

"My second announcement will be a surprise to most of you—a surprise and a shock." He paused as if to let the import of his words sink in. "Celia Lawton did not die a natural death. She was murdered."

Tom half rose from his chair. He stared at the doctor, his lips forming one terrible word, "Murdered!" That was all he said and sank back as if the life had gone out of his huge frame.

"Yes, murdered," continued the doctor grimly. "Murdered by one of you in this room."

"How do you know this? How dare you accuse one of us?" Colonel Worthington was indignant.

Dr. Bradshaw ignored the second question.

"I was not satisfied with the hasty examination I made in front of the tomb this morning. I made another after the body was brought back to the ship."

"But how was she murdered?" persisted the Colonel.

Mona was studying each face. Not a one betrayed any emotion other than surprise and a shocked interest.

"Miss Lawton was bitten by none other than the famous asp of Cleopatra, scientifically speaking, the *Cerastes cornutus*, but locally speaking, the horned viper. This snake, yellow in color like the sand, is exceedingly venomous, and is provided with a curious hornlike protuberance over each eye. She was bitten by the female viper which has two horns, both of which penetrated the flesh and injected the poison. This deadly viper causes death very quickly, the time varying with the victim's height and weight. Paralysis came upon Miss Lawton almost immediately, for when I picked her up from the floor her body was stiff and she had lost control of her muscles."

"What became of the asp?" quavered Miss Singlefoot, "I didn't see a thing that looked like a snake," under her breath she muttered a fervent, "thank goodness."

"When Miss Lawton flung the viper from her it probably crawled off into some hole in the floor or wall. Those tombs are full of crevices."

"Why didn't you tell us it was an asp's bite then?" Tom suddenly found his voice.

"I didn't discover the tell-tale mark until later. She was bitten in the left hand and that was clenched tightly together as she fell and paralysis, setting in immediately, kept it clenched. I had to pry open her hands," he concluded simply.

"Couldn't it have been an accident?" asked Jimmie. "I mean, couldn't she have run upon the snake in the tomb?"

"No," interrupted Professor Cross before the doctor could say anything. "Not in a tomb up here in the Sudan. They are seldom opened, for few people are willing to stand the hardships necessary to visiting them. Moreover, an asp is essentially a hot climate viper and it stands beyond reason that one wouldn't leave its natural home, the hot sand, to sneak off into the bowels of the earth where it is cold. Dry dust and stone walls offer no food, either, to the asp who feeds upon green leaves and bird eggs."

He turned his pale eyes on the doctor. "She was bitten in the hand you say. Then the viper must have been placed in her pocket."

"That is the way I have figured it out. As I came to the doorway of the funeral hall I looked ahead, myself, to the figure of Anubis. Miss Lawton was standing before it and I recall distinctly that she thrust her left hand down in her pocket just before she screamed. The asp must have been concealed there."

"I remember," said Sophie suddenly, "Celia was always ramming her hands down that way when she was looking at something intently. The murderer must have known it was a characteristic gesture, for obviously he made use of the knowledge to distract attention from himself. As it worked out, he was nowhere near Celia when the snake bit her."

"But when did he put it in her pocket?" asked Colonel Worthington.

"While we were walking down those dark stairs that led into the death chamber," suggested Mona.

"Or when we were in the crowd of milling donkeys and donkey boys right after we left the ship," added Jimmie. "It's always a scramble getting mounted and you sort of expect to be jostled. I think the murderer could have put the snake in any one of our pockets and we'd never have known a thing about it."

"Well, we've decided to our satisfaction that Miss Lawton was murdered," snapped Professor Cross. "What are we going to do about it?"

"We are going back to Assuan as fast as the *dahabeah* will go. There the police will come aboard and I shall turn the whole matter over to them."

"And meanwhile—?" urged the archaeologist irritably.

"Meanwhile," said the doctor as emphatically as the heat and his excessive weight would allow, "I shall make a few investigations. At the present moment we will have an informal inquest and I expect you to answer any questions that I put to you concerning the murder."

"And if we don't see fit to answer them?" said the Colonel softly.

"You will," retorted Dr. Bradshaw.

CHAPTER VII
THE ARAB OUTSIDE THE DOOR

"Mr. Amory," said Dr. Bradshaw in a firm tone, "you were closer to Miss Lawton than anyone else. I shall begin by questioning you. Are you ready?"

"Quite ready. Let's get it over as quickly as possible."

"When was the first time you ever saw Miss Lawton?"

"I met her at a dance when I was a freshman at Harvard."

"Did you continue to see her from that time on?"

"No, she left for Europe soon afterwards and it was not until three years later that I saw her again in London. I was spending my summer vacation abroad and when I discovered Celia living in an apartment in the West End I chucked all plans of touring the continent to stay near her. Since that summer, with the exception of the two years I spent in South Africa, I have been with her four or five months out of each year."

"How did you happen to take this Nile trip? It must have been a bit dull for you after your long stay in South Africa."

"No place is, or rather was, dull with Celia along. We've been planning this trip together for several years. Celia had never been beyond Cairo and the Nile always fascinated her. She used to say that the imagined fragrance of the lotus flower along the banks of the Nile was sweeter by far and more soothing to her than all the cherry blossoms of Japan. After a month in Cairo this winter she became bored and restless. She was relieved when the sailing time came. Little she knew what this trip held in store for her."

"Did you see her alone last night before she went to her cabin or this morning before she started off for the tombs?"

"I didn't see Celia to talk to her either last night or this morning. I didn't have a chance; someone else was taking up all her time." Tom glared at Spencer.

"You didn't ride along with her on the way to the tombs this morning?" Dr. Bradshaw evidently thought this was an important point.

"I did not."

"Wasn't that a bit unusual? I understood that you and Celia were engaged. Had you quarreled or disagreed over something?"

"Not exactly," said Tom, his face crimson at the memory. "At least, Celia had no part in it. As I look back on it now I feel nothing but regrets. I was simply jealous of Spencer. He kept hanging around Celia and I didn't seem to have a show with her. It hurt my pride that she preferred his company to mine. She was engaged to me, at least almost, and I felt I had some rights."

"Can you think of any reason why Miss Lawton should have been murdered? Did she have any enemies?"

"As far as I know she hadn't an enemy on earth. Women, as a whole, the jealous cats, didn't like her, but men did. She was one of the most popular women in Europe. Maybe that's the reason I never had a chance. Every time I asked her to set the date for the wedding she'd put me off, saying next year perhaps. She had a feeling that she would be giving up her freedom when she married. Lately I've gotten the idea she was waiting for something; what it was I can't say."

"How was Miss Lawton fixed financially?"

"Her father left her a very large fortune. I don't know the exact figures but I do know that she had far more than she could spend in several lifetimes. She was an extravagant person but I'm sure her income each year more than covered her demands upon it."

"Do you know whether she left a will?"

"Of course, I can't be sure but I don't think so. She told me several times she didn't believe in them. I imagine her estate will go to her two cousins. One is a newspaper man about forty or forty-five who has been in India for the past few years. The other is a young girl, twenty or thereabouts, who is still in college somewhere in the East. Celia was quite fond of her. I don't think she cared particularly for John Stewart, the newspaper man, but blood is thicker than water and she probably didn't dislike him enough to make a will preventing his inheriting in case of her death."

"Do you know John Stewart personally?"

"I just saw him a few times. He travels a lot and is seldom in Boston. I had no reason to know him intimately. Celia herself had not seen him in many years."

"Is there any information that you can add to this? I may have forgotten some point."

"I can't think of anything."

Tom had answered all these questions without a moment's hesitation, looking straight ahead as if he were alone in the room. Now he sank back into his chair, his huge frame sagging wearily. He was like a man utterly exhausted from physical labor.

"Thank you very much, Mr. Amory."

The doctor paused for a moment to take out a large pocket handkerchief. He mopped his forehead before turning to Miss Singlefoot.

"You are next," he said. "When did you become acquainted with Miss Lawton?"

"I set eyes upon Miss Lawton for the first time when I came on this Nile trip. I had never heard of her before."

"Just what was your impression of her?"

"As far as her appearance was concerned I thought she was very attractive. She certainly was pretty enough. She was sweet, too. I really can't see how anyone could have harmed her. I think it might have been an accident, anyway."

"You must get that idea out of your head, Miss Singlefoot, for it certainly was not an accident. It was premeditated murder. But to get back to the point, what did you mean by 'as far as her appearance was concerned?' Was there a side to Miss Lawton not as attractive as her personal appearance? Come, now, tell me frankly what you had in mind."

"Well, if you insist, but far be it from me to speak ill of the dead." Miss Singlefoot cleared her throat and carefully avoided Mona's eye. "As a matter of fact, I don't think it was quite proper for Miss Lawton to be traveling about the world with a man who wasn't her husband. I suppose you'll call me old-fashioned in this, but I was brought up to believe that a woman's honor comes first. Miss Lawton certainly didn't seem to care a fig for her reputation or she would have been more prudent. Since you asked me, I'm going to be honest and say what I think. Back in the States we'd call her a 'fast woman.' Mind you, I'm not saying she was one. I'm just telling you the impression she gave me. With my moral principles I could never have led the life that Miss Lawton did."

Jimmie started to make a retort to this but thought better of it.

"I am surprised at your words, Miss Singlefoot, for I'm sure I never had such an impression of Miss Lawton. However, thank you for your frankness. I appreciate your hesitation in slandering the dead." There was just the slightest tinge of sarcasm in Dr. Bradshaw's words, but if Miss Singlefoot perceived it she gave no sign, for she sat back in her chair with the pleased air of the righteous denouncing a fallen sister.

"Where is your cabin located, Miss Singlefoot?"

"Miss Lawton had the one on the end near the door and mine is right next to hers. But why in the world do you ask that?"

"I thought perhaps you could help me check up with the time Miss Lawton went to her cabin last night. Did you hear her come in?"

"I can tell exactly. I left the smoking room a little before ten o'clock and went directly down to my stateroom. Sophie—I mean Mrs. Worthington—came by my room a few minutes later for her Baedeker that I had borrowed. We were standing in the door when we saw Miss Lawton going to her room. She was smiling and humming a tune. Mrs. Worthington looked at her watch and remarked that it was just ten-fifteen, and unusually early for Miss Lawton to be retiring." Miss Singlefoot glanced at Sophie, who nodded her head in confirmation.

"Now, Miss Singlefoot, I want you to think carefully before you answer my next question. Did you hear anything during the night that might bear on the murder?" Dr. Bradshaw looked straight at Miss Singlefoot, who hesitated for a moment.

"No, I did not," she said finally.

"Are you sure?"

"I'm sure."

"You're next, then, Colonel Worthington," continued Dr. Bradshaw, turning to the Englishman. "Had you ever met Miss Lawton before you came on this trip?"

"Yes, she made my wife a short visit this fall in England. Miss Lawton was really the one who persuaded us to come to Egypt. At that time she gave me the impression of being a very gay sort of person who followed the seasons around all over Europe. She and my wife knew each other when they were schoolgirls. I think they were together for a while in New York, too."

"That's interesting. Perhaps Mrs. Worthington can be of great help to us. By the way, what is your occupation? Have you always led such a leisurely life?"

"Up to two years ago I was a colonel in the English army. Since then I've been on the retired list."

"If it's not inquiring too much into your private affairs, will you tell me why you are retired at your age? Forty-five is a bit young for retirement."

"Why, certainly. I have no objection whatever. I was stationed five years in India and while there contracted a tropical disease which, though not contagious or deadly, nevertheless prevents my living the hard life of a soldier. Since then I've been taking it easy, devoting most of my time to managing the estate left to me by my father."

"Do you know of any reason that would account for Miss Lawton's death? Do you have any theories regarding the murder?"

"None whatever."

"Do you believe that Celia feared anyone? Or to put it differently, did she have an inkling of what was going to happen to her?"

"As far as I know, she didn't have a care in the world. I've heard her say that she was afraid of nothing. No, I don't think she had any foreboding of the future."

"Thank you, Colonel Worthington. That will be all for the present."

The man relaxed perceptibly as the doctor turned his attention to Sophie Worthington.

"And now, Mrs. Worthington, if you will be so kind as to answer a few questions. You alone out of the group knew Miss Lawton when she was young. Perhaps you can tell us the reason why she was murdered." Dr. Bradshaw's voice was gentle and it was quite evident that he liked this blue-eyed woman. She was attractive with her voluptuous curves and blonde hair.

"I'm afraid I can add very little to what's already been said. How-ever, in my estimation Celia has always played with fire and though I had not expected her violent death, now that it has happened I am not a bit surprised."

"What do you mean by 'playing with fire'?"

"I don't know that I can put it into words exactly, but all her life Celia has had one heavy beau after another. She would accept the attentions of one man for a while and then suddenly for no apparent reason refuse to see him any more. She was fickle and utterly care-less of how many hearts she broke. Of course, I haven't seen a great deal of her in the last five years, but from past experience and from what I've heard about her since I left America she hasn't changed any of her ways."

"So you think she might have been murdered by some disap-pointed lover?"

"I can't think of any other reason. A person who has no regard for other people's opinions and feelings might as well expect to get theirs in the end."

"I am under the impression that you were on the stage before you lived in London. Am I right, Mrs. Worthington?"

"How in the world did you guess? My husband didn't volunteer that bit of information, did he?" The dry humor in her voice indicat-ed that Colonel Worthington would be reluctant at any time to speak of his wife's stage career.

"Oh, not at all. It was a chance question which I see happened to hit the mark. Besides, Mrs. Worthington, with your beauty and natural histrionic ability one would always be justified in asking such a question."

The woman's bright red lips curved into a smile.

"As a matter of fact," she said, "I was on the stage for a few years before I married. I played in several of Flo Ziegfeld's shows."

"Were you brought up in New York, Mrs. Worthington?"

"No, when I was young I lived in Kingston, a small town on the Hudson. When I was eighteen my father, who was a doctor, sent me to New York to take a course of training as a nurse. I didn't like the work and at the first chance I gave it up and went in for dancing."

"Was Miss Lawton in New York during your stage career?"

"She was there for two years."

"Did anything happen then that might have the slightest bearing on her murder?"

"No, not to my knowledge."

"Do you know either of Miss Lawton's cousins?"

"I know John Stewart."

"Do you agree with Mr. Amory that Miss Lawton and Mr. Stewart were not very congenial?"

"Yes."

"Thank you, Mrs. Worthington. That will be all."

He cleared his throat noisily.

"Professor Cross, you're next. Did you know the deceased before you came aboard this boat?"

"No, I did not."

"What time did you go to your cabin last night?"

"I went down with most of the others a little before ten."

"Did you leave it for anything during the night?"

"No."

"Whom did you ride with on your way to the tombs this morning?"

"Mrs. Worthington and I rode along together."

"Is there any information that you can give me concerning Miss Lawton's murder?"

"I am sorry to say there is none. Her death came to me as a shock and certainly a complete surprise." Professor Cross spoke slowly in the manner of a man who is accustomed to weighing each word carefully.

At this moment the clanging sound of the luncheon gong was heard and it accentuated the restlessness of the group.

"We will meet again later in the day," said Dr. Bradshaw. "Perhaps, though," he amended, thoughtfully, "on account of the heat I'll question Mr. Spencer and Mr. Bean in my office and I won't bother the others. I'll let them know when I want them."

They rose to go. It had been a long, hot session and weariness was written on each face.

"Oh, Miss Case," called Dr. Bradshaw as he followed her out on the sun-blistered deck. She waited for him and he lowered his voice as he spoke again.

"Did you get anything out of all the questioning?"

"Not much," she said. "I'm wondering, though, what part was of especial interest to Abdu, the room steward?"

"Abdu?" asked the doctor in astonishment.

"Yes, Abdu. He was flattened against the wall just outside the door during the whole inquest."

CHAPTER VIII
STARING EYES

Miss Singlefoot was dressed for dinner. She made a point of it while traveling. She never had a chance at home. That was the nice thing about English boats. People always dressed for dinner on them. Come storms, come groundings, come murders, the entire passenger list was found in evening clothes by seven o'clock.

It was not quite seven when Miss Singlefoot left her cabin. Too early for dinner. No one would be in the dining room at this hour. What should she do for the next ten minutes? Perhaps Professor Cross was up on deck waiting too. If so, they could have a chat together. He was such a clever man; he might be able to tell her who killed Miss Lawton. Anyway, he'd probably have some good idea about it. She liked quiet, forceful men like Professor Cross.

She went up on the sun deck. That was where he'd be if he were already dressed. It was not so hot and stuffy there. This was the only pretty time of the day. You never thought of the beauty of nature at noon in Africa. You only wished for a miracle to drench the earth in blessed coolness.

But Professor Cross was not to be found. She had no one with whom she could enjoy the first hush of the evening. How disappointing!

She leaned over the taffrail. All was quiet and peaceful. Her thoughts turned to that still room below. It would be quiet down there, too. A deadly quiet.

What was that she heard? A light buzzing which seemed to grow fiercer. It annoyed her. Where was it coming from?

She turned around to peer at the whiteness of the wall behind her. Whiteness broken by a black hole that was the head of the aft-stairway. The sound was coming from that direction. Like static on a radio. But what was it? She left the rail to investigate the closet beside the stairs.

Flies! Thousands of flies buzzing and hissing in the semi-darkness. Flies that sounded like bees. That was it. Bees. But why so many? Bees live in a hive. The top of the door reminded her of the beehives at home.

All the doors on the ship were like that. The lower half was solid but the top was like a shutter. It was on account of the heat.

Heat. Heat and noise in the quiet of the evening. Irritating. What were the flies doing there? What was behind that shutter?

She'd see. Probably those lazy Arab waiters had put the unwashed tea dishes there. It would be just like them. A lazy trifling lot. All of them. Nosy, too. Especially the room steward.

She turned the knob. It wouldn't budge. Everything stuck on the *Assuit*. She gave a jerk. The door flew open. The knob slipped from her limp fingers.

She didn't remember screaming. They told her afterwards that she did. A terrible scream that rocked the little boat from stern to bow.

She only remembered standing there staring. Staring into white eyes. Eyes that held hers in a hypnotic grasp. Eyes that gleamed white out of a black face.

A black face. A white robe. There was some color. What was it? Oh yes, a green belt. Of course. It was Abdu, the room steward. He had been to Mecca. All Mohammedans who had been to Mecca wore green belts. It was supposed to mean something. Just what, she couldn't remember.

Something moved on his face. A fly. Two of them. Why didn't he brush them away?

She laughed shrilly, hysterically. That was a silly question. Very silly.

He was dead and the dead don't feel flies. The dead only stare.

People were swarming around her. Like flies and bees.

"I thought it was a beehive," she said and laughed again.

Mona was talking to her. She was holding something to her lips. She kept saying, "Swallow this and you'll feel better. Swallow."

It burnt her tongue. She could feel it going down her throat. How warm it felt in her stomach. She hadn't realized how cold she was. But how could she be cold? This was a hot boat.

What was she worrying about? Something was pounding in her head. She wished it would stop. Worrying. If she could just think without that pounding. It was Abdu, the room steward. The nosy one. He worried her. What made him stare so?

It wasn't dark now. She was in her cabin. She could hear noises above her. Someone was walking heavily on the thin floor. Perhaps they were carrying something. Dead weight. You walked heavily when you carried dead weight.

"Why did he stare so, Mona?"

"Who, dear?"

"Abdu."

"He was dead. You forget it, though, and rest awhile."

But she didn't want to rest. She wanted to talk. She wanted to talk about Abdu. Dead Abdu and his staring eyes.

So many were dead. First, Miss Lawton. She stared, too. She stared before she was dead. Maybe she was staring now in her cabin. But no one saw her.

They would lock Abdu in a cabin. He couldn't stare at people any more. He would be like Miss Lawton. Dead and staring at the ceiling.

"I hope no one else is dead," she said. "I don't like dead people. They stare too much."

CHAPTER IX
BLOOD ON THE WINDING

Jack Spencer was helping Dr. Bradshaw carry the body downstairs. The Arabs wouldn't touch it. They stood in a frightened huddle watching the procedure.

"We'll take it to that empty room next to my office," panted the doctor.

"Have you the key?" Spencer's voice came in little jerks. Damned heavy, this Arab. He was carrying the weighty part, anyway—the head and shoulders.

"Unlocked," was the only answer.

They laid the body on the bed.

"No wonder Miss Singlefoot screamed," said Spencer. "It's not pleasant looking at a dead man any time, much less at one standing up." He stopped suddenly as an idea occurred to him. "By George, I hadn't thought of that. Standing up! How could he have been standing up?"

"He wasn't really. Whoever put him in the closet left him crumpled against a stack of life preservers. As you can see, he was nearly seven feet tall—his height coupled with the rigidity of the body after the muscles stiffened gave him the appearance of standing and brought his eyes to the level of a man of ordinary height. Miss Singlefoot, though tall for a woman, probably without realizing it, looked down a bit instead of straight into his face."

Spencer nodded his head. "You sure can't blame her for being frightened. His eyes are enough to shock the bravest."

"We'll end their staring." The doctor took off his coat and rolled up his shirt sleeves. "Let's see what killed him, anyway."

He closed the eyes and began a thorough examination. There was silence for a few moments as the doctor, plump and perspiring, puttered over the body. Spencer stood beside him, his dark eyes watching every move.

"There are marks about the throat—deep bruises in the muscles. Probably made by the grip of strong fingers."

"He was strangled then?"

"No, I don't think so. The marks look like they were made after death, perhaps by dragging the body. Besides, his lips are not those of a strangled man. Neither are his eyes. They are wide and staring but not bulging. They would have bulged if he had been choked."

"It must be hard to choke an Arab to death," commented Spencer, looking down at his own hands doubtfully. They were strong and long fingered. "Arabs have such thick, tough necks."

"Hump," muttered the doctor almost to himself. Dead bodies. Strange murders. Always hard to find the cause. This man did not die by an asp's bite. There were no two little marks and no swelling.

"Here, help me turn him over. Maybe the attack came from behind. You will note his clothes are not rumpled. There probably wasn't much of a struggle."

It was a hard job. The body seemed to have taken on more weight. The room was hot. A few fireflies, hovering around the speckled light bulb, beat it noisily with their wings.

"Did we do that?" demanded Spencer suddenly pointing down at the back of the dead man's head.

"What?" asked the doctor, mechanically wiping the perspiration off his forehead with his shirt sleeve. He saw nothing unusual.

"Why, his turban is pulled too low on his neck. There's very little skin showing."

"Damn queer. Wait. I'll take it off." He began unwinding the white headcloth. Suddenly he nodded his head approvingly.

"Blood," he whispered. "Blood. We're getting somewhere."

Spencer leaned over the doctor's shoulder. About every thirty inches on the white band was a tiny round bloodstain. As the winding got closer to the end the stains were larger and a deeper crimson.

Dr. Bradshaw laid aside the turban and examined the neck.

"That's what got him," he said and pointed to a small, blood-clotted hole about the size of a baby pea. It was where the hair ceased to grow on the back of the neck.

"By George, you're right."

"He was struck by some small, sharp instrument, the point of which pierced the spinal column just at the base of the brain. He died instantly."

"It must have taken a strong arm," suggested Spencer.

"Not necessarily. Any ordinary man could have done it, provided he knew where to strike. A strong woman could have, too, for that matter."

"Poor devil," mused Spencer. "He never knew what hit him."

They turned the body on its back.

"How long has he been dead, doctor?"

"I can't be exact but, all things considered, I should say from four to six hours."

"Terrible the way those flies spotted the body, wasn't it? It gave me a turn. What do you suppose it all means? First Miss Lawton and now Abdu."

"I don't know," answered the doctor wearily.

"Is there no way of getting aid from the police before we reach Assuan?"

"No way at all."

Spencer stared at the doctor with growing apprehension. His dry lips moved slowly.

"This boat isn't safe. We're liable to be knifed in our beds."

"We shall have to keep our doors locked. Everyone is in danger. Even you and I."

The two men looked into each other's horror-stricken eyes.

"Come, I must warn the other passengers," said the doctor finally, putting on his coat. His fingers closed upon something in his pocket before he continued. "From now on, no one is safe."

He locked the door upon the second dead body.

CHAPTER X
THE LISTENER IN WHITE

"I have just had a little talk with Mr. Spencer," said the doctor, offering Mona a cigarette. "He has known Miss Lawton a long time. Said he first met her at Monte Carlo in 1920 at a gambling table."

"Celia spoke of him as an old friend. What else did he have to say?"

"Nothing much. The two seem to have been visiting the same winter resorts almost regularly each year. Spencer claims they were not in love with each other but simply found it amusing to play around together."

"Did you ask him if he thought Celia feared violence from anyone?"

"He said he felt certain that she had no fear of death—that she lived too hard and ruthlessly to have time for morbid forebodings."

"Ruthlessly," repeated Mona. "I wonder what he meant by that?"

"I asked him but he just smiled and made some noncommittal reply."

"Sophie Worthington used practically the same word when she spoke of Celia. Perhaps it was some ruthless thing she had done which caused her death."

"Perhaps. Spencer admitted to having been with Miss Lawton this morning from the time she mounted her donkey until we entered the tomb. I told him that he had a very good opportunity to put the snake in her pocket. He didn't seem a bit perturbed at the suggestion."

"Did you find out what he does for a living?"

"Yes. He is the foreign agent for a bond company in Rochester, New York."

"What time did he go to his cabin last night?"

"About ten o'clock. He dropped Tom by his door and then went on to his own."

"Did you get anything else from him?"

"Not a thing."

"Humph," said Mona in disgust. "According to everyone's story no one killed Celia. Yet somebody did. And Abdu. He has to be accounted for."

"I questioned Jimmie Bean, too, but he was no help at all. He had never met Miss Lawton before this trip and had seen very little of her on it. So far, we haven't gotten near the solution of this mess."

"We might have," said Mona thoughtfully, "if Abdu hadn't been killed."

"Abdu? Do you think he knew the secret?"

"I do. I think that is why he died. You see, he was the room steward and probably discovered something that looked suspicious in one of the cabins. Then Celia died and no cause was given for her death. He was curious when you called a meeting of the passengers and so listened at the door. No doubt his death is a result of what he overheard in that meeting."

"He knew too much for the killer's safety."

"Exactly."

"That's why, Miss Case, I can't let you try to discover the murderer. It's dangerous and you're too young to be involved in such hazardous business."

"You must have been talking to Jimmie about me. He said the same thing. But why should anyone know about it? I made Jimmie promise not to tell."

"We are dealing with an unscrupulous criminal who is, first of all, a careful observer of details. Both murders show that trait in him. He's going to be on the lookout for anyone snooping about. If you were to discover something you might not live to disclose it."

"We are wasting time," said Mona determinedly. "I'm twenty-five, and my own boss. If I get killed 'snooping,' as you put it, it's no one's fault but my own."

"I shall speak to your aunt," warned the doctor.

"Don't," advised Mona gravely. "She might tell the murderer unintentionally. She has a habit of talking a great deal and she likes Professor Cross too much."

"Professor Cross?" Dr. Bradshaw did not voice the question his tone implied.

"I don't like Professor Cross. His eyes are too cold and fish-like."

"Fishy eyes are not necessarily the prerequisite of a murderer. Anything else against him?"

"Not yet. Will you do something for me, Dr. Bradshaw?"

"What is it?"

"I want you to talk to all the passengers in the dining room to-morrow morning after breakfast. You can discuss the murder with them or ask them some more questions—anything, just so you keep them there for twenty minutes."

"That is a strange request. What's the idea behind it?"

"I want to search the cabins. You could do it yourself officially, but I think the result would be better if it were done without their knowledge."

"But how will you get in? I told them to lock their cabins."

"Only at night. There'd be no reason to lock them in the daytime when everyone is on deck. The danger is physical and to their person, not their belongings. There has been no theft."

"And if I don't promise to do this?"

"I'll search the cabins anyway and the murderer might catch me at it."

"I'll keep them in the dining room," said the doctor grimly.

"Don't be despondent about it," admonished Mona with a half-smile. "I'm the logical person to spot the murderer, for I'm the one he'd suspect least. Most young women hate this sort of thing. He doesn't know I'm an ex-newspaper woman who has reported many a murder trial."

Dr. Bradshaw was looking for his pipe. He hunted in his desk drawer, on the shelf, and finally in his coat pockets. He didn't find the pipe but he did find something else he had momentarily forgotten. It was a little white piece of paper with one side a ragged edge. He handed it to Mona.

"Just what would you say that is?" he asked.

Mona examined it carefully.

"Looks like the end of a bank note."

"Exactly. A five-pound one."

"Where did you get it?"

"It was clutched tightly in Abdu's right hand. I found it when I was examining the body. Spencer was with me and I very carefully concealed it from him."

"Somehow I don't think Spencer did it. He is too nice."

Dr. Bradshaw smiled.

"You are the detective on the case," he said, "but take a little advice from the doctor, also, on the case. Don't for one moment think that a murderer is necessarily a stupid or an unattractive person. He may be a fiend, and perhaps not normal when he's taking another's life, but on the other hand, he may be the most plausible, the most entertaining person imaginable."

Mona wasn't listening. She was staring through the crack in the door that gave her a view of the stairway just outside the doctor's office. Holding her fingers to her lips she got up from her chair, and pushed the door back gently, but not gently enough, for its hinges, outraged by violent changes of temperature, creaked loudly. The sound was enough to frighten away the wearer of white who had been listening intently on the steps.

CHAPTER XI
HANDS OUT OF THE DARK

Mona refused Dr. Bradshaw's offer to accompany her to her cabin.

"I'm not scared," she said, "and even if I were I wouldn't admit it. Besides, the decks have lights, such as they are."

"Well, good night then. Be sure to lock your door securely. I've no doubt you caught a glimpse of the murderer on the steps. That means he knows what you're up to. You must be terribly careful. I wish I could do something to insure your safety." He shook his head helplessly. "But I don't even have an extra gun."

"Perhaps we won't need one. Good night, Doctor." She started for her cabin slowly. It was up on the next deck at the extreme end of the *dahabeah*.

A strange quiet pervaded the corridor outside the doctor's office. The very atmosphere itself seemed still as if all life had gone elsewhere for its sustenance. Only the deep shadows in the well of the stairway appeared to move and beckon grotesquely. As Mona began her ascent, with her hands on the banisters, she peered into the semi-darkness, as if hopeful of piercing its obscurity and yet fearful of what she might discover. There was no sound except the noise made by her leather heels striking against the wooden steps. The words of a poem flitted through her mind. "I feel like one who treads alone some banquet hall deserted, whose lights are fled, whose garlands dead and all but he departed." She shivered apprehensively while her silent lips formed a question. Were there other murders yet to come? If so, who would be the next victim? It was hellish, this prying into the future, this foreseeing danger and not being able to prevent it.

The machinery of her brain began to work again. Cool reasoning usurped fantastic shadows. Both murders had been done cleanly, the instrument of death in each case being missing. Celia was killed by an asp, but what was used to kill Abdu? Something long, sharp and small in circumference. What could it have been?

Mona's thoughts went back to the day the *Assuit* sailed. Did the temporarily missing bag and the permanently missing soap box have anything to do with these two murders? And what relation did Aunt Ella have with it all?

She stopped dead in her tracks. Aunt Ella! Was she to be the third victim? But no, that was silly. Who would kill such a harmless soul? She was a bit queer and old-fashioned where morals were concerned but, after all, she was a dear about most things.

"What in the world!" muttered Mona to herself in surprise. "Who turned off the lights?"

She was standing at the top of the stairs about twenty feet from the door opening on a passageway that led to her cabin. Not a light was burning on that side of the deck.

"Maybe the Arab forgot them in the excitement," she continued to herself, in a vain attempt to bolster up her courage. "Let's see, now, where is the switch?"

She started feeling her way along the wall that led to the passage doorway. The switches were there. It was beastly dark. Africa could be so bright in the day and so black at night. She could not shake off the coldness settling on her spine. Why hadn't she let Dr. Bradshaw come with her? She hated darkness—and this was so thick and oppressive.

Ah, here was the doorway. She felt the casement thankfully. No light burned in the passage. Damn that Arab. Nothing but darkness. What if someone lurked there, waiting for her? It might have been the murderer who turned off the lights. The thought choked her.

She touched the door itself. It was half open. The switches were just inside on the right. She felt for them, her fingers moving uncertainly along the wall.

Suddenly she heard a rustle. The door moved behind her back. She tried to scream but her tongue was frozen to the roof of her mouth. She felt hot breath on her neck as she lunged blindly toward the switches.

Strong hands were around her throat. They were squeezing tightly, so tightly. She tried to push them away. Little red balls were burning in front of her eyes. Her knees were giving way beneath her. It was terribly dark. The ghastly realization of what was happening flashed through her stunned brain. Her senses reeled. These were the murderer's hands and she was the third victim.

Eternity had passed. It was still dark but the hands were gone. Those horrible choking hands. She was on the floor. She was not dead. Perhaps the murderer was still there, gloating in the darkness.

She screamed loudly. It hurt her throat but she screamed again and again. A rush of footsteps rewarded her efforts.

"Where are you?" someone called. It sounded like Tom.

"Here by the switches." Her voice was weak and her legs crumpled ineffectually beneath her as she tried to pull herself up.

"My child, what's the matter? What happened?" Dr. Bradshaw had turned on the lights and was kneeling beside her.

Mona pointed to her throat. Faint marks showed through the skin.

"Something—somebody—out of the darkness choked me."

She looked up at the crowd. They were standing around her, solicitude written on their faces. Jack and Tom, Sophie and her husband, Jimmie and Aunt Ella. Where was Professor Cross? Oh, there he was at the back. He smiled at her, a cold, crooked smile. She shuddered.

But he couldn't be the murderer. The murderer wore white and Professor Cross's clothes were black.

It was Tom. He had on a white linen suit. But so did Jack, and Colonel Worthington and Jimmie. Even Sophie beneath her black wrap wore a white dress. And Aunt Ella—she must have rushed from her bed for she knelt there shivering in a white silken wrapper.

It was hopeless. They were all in white except Professor Cross.

She was carried to the smoking room.

"Drink this," said the doctor, handing her a pony of whiskey.

Mona noticed vaguely that his white uniform was rumpled.

She drank slowly. Swallowing was difficult. How her throat ached!

She set the glass on the edge of the table. With a crash it fell to the floor.

Professor Cross leaned over and picked up the broken pieces.

"Sorry," said Mona softly.

"Quite all right," he returned.

But was it? Professor Cross wore white socks. She had seen them when he bent over.

CHAPTER XII
CAT'S EYES

"One of you in this room is the murderer," said Dr. Bradshaw with conviction. "I have searched the ship from top to bottom and proven to my own satisfaction that no person unaccounted for is aboard the *Assuit*. Therefore, the murderer is not a stowaway. The other possibility, that of an Arab servant, is remote. I cross-examined the members of the crew, however, but as far as I was concerned my effort was wasted. They not only appeared to know nothing of the murder but were so frightened by the happenings that their answers were incoherent and practically meaningless. Besides with the English rule what it is in Egypt and the Sudan, any native would be mortally afraid of killing a foreigner—especially an Englishwoman or an American. Yes, I think we can count an Arab out as the potential murderer. The search must be confined to the passenger list."

"How about yourself, Doctor?" asked Colonel Worthington bluntly. "Why couldn't you have killed her?"

Dr. Bradshaw stared at him in surprise.

"I would have no motive," he said quickly. "I never saw Miss Lawton before three days ago."

"That's your story," retorted Colonel Worthington.

The doctor was highly indignant. His face was crimson and he glared at the Colonel for a moment quite as if he would like to strike him. Then he became calm, though his pudgy hands continued to twitch nervously. He was like a balloon that had suddenly been punctured.

"Perhaps you are right," he said with no heat in his voice. "From now on I shall say 'one of us is the murderer.'"

Mona was watching all their faces, searching for some sign—some involuntary betrayal of guilt. But the criminal had a close grip on himself.

"I know I shan't sleep another wink until we're back to civilization." Miss Singlefoot's voice was shrill. "The murderer must be a lunatic. Why should he be choking Mona? He'll be grabbing hold of me next and the Lord knows he won't have to grab hard. I think I'd die in my tracks if someone yelled 'boo' at me." She stood beside her niece's chair, her wrapper pulled tightly around her thin frame, her hair disheveled from sleeping. In the excitement she was unaware of the figure she cut.

"Well, if one of us is the murderer and the murderer choked Mona less than ten minutes ago it ought to be easy to spot him." Spencer looked around the group thoughtfully. "Just where was each one of you when you heard the scream?"

"I was in the library," said Professor Cross, and added succinctly, "alone."

"What did you do when you heard the scream?"

"I jumped from my chair and ran out into the corridor in the direction of the noise. Naturally."

"You were the last one to arrive. I noticed that," persisted Spencer pointedly. "Why?"

"Perhaps, I don't run as fast as you," returned Professor Cross quite as pointedly. "Where were you when Miss Case screamed?"

"I was playing cards in this room with Jimmie and Colonel Worthington. We three ran out together."

"All accounted for," said Dr. Bradshaw, "except Mr. Amory and Mrs. Worthington."

"Don't forget yourself," reminded the Englishman.

"And myself," repeated the doctor dryly. "I mustn't forget that I'm a suspect. At the time Miss Case screamed I was in the stern talking to the sailors. They are threatening mutiny again. Abdu's death, probably because he was of their kind, upset them even more than Miss Lawton's. They are genuinely frightened, not of anything physical but of the supernatural. They say an evil spirit has put a curse on this boat. And as for the two corpses—why, I honestly believe they'd have me chuck them overboard into the river. They'd do it themselves only none of them would dare touch a dead body."

"The curse of an evil spirit," Professor Cross repeated softly. "I suppose they warned you of even more evil to come."

"They did," replied the doctor, "and I showed them I was ready for it." He pulled an ugly looking Colt from his pocket. "At the first suspicious move from anyone I'm going to shoot. And I shoot straight," he added grimly.

"I say, we're forgetting Tom. Where were you, old boy, when Mona screamed?" Spencer smoothed down his slick black hair. He looked at Tom intently.

"I know this sounds fishy," said Tom slowly, "but I was sitting on the front deck doing nothing. It was quiet there and I wanted to think."

"You didn't have a coat on? It's too cool at nine o'clock to sit motionless on deck."

"I didn't feel the cold," returned Tom.

"No, you probably didn't," sneered Colonel Worthington. "We've all got alibis but you and you don't even tell a plausible story."

"Professor Cross had no alibi either," remarked Jimmie thoughtfully.

"No, but he hadn't any motive for the murder that I can see. Tom had one. A good one too. He was jealous as hell. Anybody could see that. And Tom knows a lot about snakes. He wasn't an engineer in Africa two years for nothing. A man can learn a lot in that time."

"And so could you in India," retorted Tom. "You were there five years. I get your idea all right—trying to pin the murder on me. You didn't exactly hate Celia yourself. I've seen you talking to her a lot—too darn much."

"For goodness sakes, let's don't start another argument," snapped Sophie fiercely. She put her hands to her temples. "This thing is driving me mad—absolutely mad." Her last word was almost a shriek.

Mona glanced at her in surprise. She did look tired. The expression about her eyes was strained.

"Where were you when I screamed?" asked Mona suddenly.

"Where was I? Sitting there by the light reading while the men were playing cards at the other end of the room."

"What did you do when you heard the scream?"

"I ran right out into the corridor. I remember hearing the bridge players push back their chairs. I was nearest the door so I got away first."

Mona looked at Sophie's strong, white hands. A huge green emerald blinked at her ominously.

"The murderer," she said, "wore no rings."

"But none of us men wear rings," said Jimmie. "That won't help any."

Mona was silent for a moment. That emerald ring reminded her of something. What was it? She remembered suddenly. A cat with very green eyes had scratched her once in the dark. It was when she was a child, playing hide-and-seek. The emerald might have been one of those cat's eyes, petrified. Rubbish, what a silly thought. But she didn't like emeralds. She wouldn't wear one. It was bad luck. Sophie was foolish to take a chance.

"I see you are wearing an emerald," Mona nodded to Sophie's hand. "Emeralds are bad luck."

"Oh, I'm not superstitious," replied Sophie lightly. "Besides, you are thinking of opals."

"I'd take it off anyway," said Colonel Worthington shortly. "This is one time you don't want to be unlucky. To be unlucky might mean—" He hesitated.

"That I'd be the third victim." Sophie looked down at the emerald, a frown between her eyes. "I shouldn't like that," she said, but did not remove the ring. Instead she turned it around slowly on her third finger. A slight red mark was noticeable just above the middle joint. "It is tight," she explained, "this hot weather. But I think I shall continue to wear it. I'm used to it."

Mona was feeling almost normal again. The whiskey had done that.

"I'm so sorry I disturbed your bridge game," she apologized. "Who was winning the rubber?"

"Oh, we weren't playing bridge," answered Jimmie. "We were playing rummy. There were just three of us, you see."

"I'm going to bed," Miss Singlefoot broke into the conversation suddenly. "If I stay here any longer I'll catch my death of cold and if I go downstairs I'll probably be knifed in the back or bitten by a snake. But I'm going just the same. And you are going with me, Mona, to my cabin. I won't have you spending the night away off up there on the sun deck."

"A good idea," approved Dr. Bradshaw. "None of us must take the slightest risk. This is no longer a pleasure boat."

"Pleasure boat," snorted Jimmie. "This is a floating morgue."

"On the River Styx with our busy Captain playing the boatman Charon," added Professor Cross sardonically.

"There is a murderer among us," continued the doctor, disregarding the comparison. "He may not be literally a maniac but his mind is terribly distorted at times. You must lock your doors and keep them locked until broad daylight. Good night, all of you, and I hope to God nothing happens before morning."

"Amen," muttered Miss Singlefoot as she and Mona led the way to the cabins below.

Only one person on board did not fear death that night. And that person was the murderer.

CHAPTER XIII
FOOTSTEPS THAT DISAPPEAR

Tom sat bolt upright in bed. The click of metal against metal had awakened him out of a light sleep.

"Who's there?" he called.

No answer.

"Who's there?" he called again, feeling for the light switch. Silence and darkness mocked him. What was wrong with the lights anyway? A fuse must have blown out. He couldn't remember what he'd done with his torch.

Another sound came from the hall. Tom bounded to the floor. As he reached for the door knob his hand brushed against the key which he had left in the lock. To his astonishment he felt it turn. Someone on the other side of the door was manipulating the key on the inside. He would have sworn he heard a chuckle and footsteps. God, if he just had a gun. He wasn't afraid without one in the light but in the dark he'd have no chance unarmed.

A door closed down the hall. Tom turned the knob slowly. The lock did not give. Evidently the person who had been trying to enter his room had heard him get out of bed. The relocking of the door was done to gain time for the intruder to escape.

Tom decided suddenly that a little light would be the better part of valor. He thought of the candle on the shelf. He had noticed it while unpacking. Ah, there it was. Now, where in blazes were the matches? He remembered some in the pocket of the suit he'd been wearing. He'd have to find his trousers. He fumbled about in the darkness for the chair. If only he had his hands on the fellow who turned out those lights! The trousers had slipped from the

chair to the floor and a box of matches was in the pocket just as
he thought.

The tallow sputtered feebly in the black stillness of the little
room. Tom caught a shadowy glimpse of himself in the mirror. God!
how haggard and disheveled he looked, standing there holding a
candle in his shaking hand. This tub! What had Jimmie called it? "A
floating morgue!" It was worse than that. A floating hell.

Muttering to himself he put on his bathrobe and slippers. Who
in the dickens was monkeying around his room? The grimness about
his eyes increased as he unlocked the door.

No one was in the hall. The candle lighted it only in spots. Tom
explored from one end to the other. The bottoms of his house shoes
made a queer little slapping sound when he walked.

His room was at the end of the hall. It was across from Celia's old
room—the room in which Celia's body lay now. He stood outside the
door listening. No sound came from within. None would, of course.
Celia, his Celia was dead. The dead make no sound. A feeling of lone-
liness swept over him, standing there in the semi-darkness.

He looked down the corridor. Closed doors. Who was awake behind those doors? Who was standing with his ear pressed against
wood, listening even as he was listening?

Was it Jack Spencer? Jack was all right on the surface but there
might very well be something behind all that plausibility. Was he the
murderer? Was he the night prowler? Were they one and the same?

Tom knocked softly on his door.

"Jack," he called.

No answer. He knocked again and louder. Hot tallow dripped on
his bare hand. He almost dropped the candle.

"Jack, old man!"

A muffled sound came from within and then a sleepy voice.

"Who's there?"

"It's Tom. Let me in."

Two bare feet hit the floor. Tom heard the scratch of a match being lighted. Someone was standing behind the locked door, breathing heavily.

"What's the matter?" drifted sleepily through the night.

"Have you heard any noises?"

"No, I've been asleep. Have you?"

"Someone tried to get in my room. I heard him at the lock."

Shadows were closing in on Tom.

"Are you sure?"

"Of course," snapped Tom. Why didn't Jack open the door?

There was a sound of the light switch being turned, to no purpose and a muttered curse.

"It's no use," offered Tom, in a matter-of-fact voice. "The current's out."

"Hell, what's the idea? More funny business?"

"Looks like it."

"Well, I, for one, am not going to unlock my door until daylight. I don't trust anybody in the dark—not as long as Dr. Bradshaw is the only one with a gun."

Silence followed this admission.

"Don't blame you," said Tom. "It may have been nothing but my imagination anyway. I'm jumpy as an old woman."

"Good night, then. See you in the morning." From the sounds that came through the door Jack was evidently stumbling across the floor to bed.

A frown wrinkled Tom's forehead into a grimace. Funny that Jack didn't try to turn on the lights when he first awakened. He had lighted a match instead. Did he know the lights were off? And was he just pretending later that he didn't know it? His voice sounded relieved too when he said "good night." Was Jack busy with some nocturnal adventure of his own? And if so, what was it?

Suddenly a little ray of light filtered into the hall. It was coming from under the door of the second room on the left. Colonel Worthington's room. Why wasn't he asleep? Tom knocked on his door which was immediately opened—just a crack though.

"It's Tom Amory. I heard strange noises and got up to investigate."

"Noises? What kind?"

"Someone tried to work the lock to my room. What are you doing up?"

"I was nervous and couldn't sleep, so I thought I'd read for a while. Just as I started on a story the lights went out. I sat here in the dark a few minutes thinking they would come on again. But they didn't. I had decided to go back to bed when I heard a commotion in the hall. I made a light and was about to investigate when you knocked. I guess it was you I heard. What do you think has happened to the electricity?"

"I don't know," Tom spoke slowly. He was staring at the man's head.

"Good night, Colonel Worthington," he said mechanically.

The door closed softly in his face. He stood still for a moment, the hot tallow falling unnoticed on the front of his dressing gown.

Colonel Worthington said he had tried to sleep and couldn't—that he was restless, and yet, on his head the hair was neatly brushed just as if he'd never been to bed.

CHAPTER XIV
WHAT THE FELUCCA HELD

Mona spent a restless night. She dreamed of big black spiders claw-ing at her neck and racing down her spine. Miss Singlefoot had her troubles too. In the early hours of the morning she rose up in bed screaming "murder" at the top of her voice, and then fell back on the pillows sighing heavily. Mona was awakened later by the sound of someone walking. She lay on the couch, paralyzed with fright until it occurred to her who it was. Miss Singlefoot was stalking up and down the floor moaning softly to herself. Another nightmare.

Needless to say, Mona was glad to see the first rays of light steal-ing through her window. Half an hour later she was up and dressed. She felt wretched. Her neck was sore and deep black bruises remind-ed her of how near death she had been the night before.

Her breakfast was a solitary meal for she wanted to be finished and ready to search the cabins by the time the other passengers were in the dining salon. Sophie usually breakfasted in her cabin but she'd probably join the crowd this morning. No one cared about being left alone even for half an hour.

The top deck was empty. Mona stood by the rail on the river side. The sun was up and its rays, already beginning to show signs of heat, promised a scorching day to come. The boat was moving slow-ly through the thick, muddy water which lapped the sun-cracked wood resentfully. Several little feluccas tied to the large boat scraped against its creaking sides harshly. Hangers-on, thought Mona, are never pleasant.

Abruptly her thought left the swishing water below. They went to the silent cabin where Celia lay stiff and cold. Mona had stood beside the bed before Dr. Bradshaw locked the door. She had looked down upon that still, white face and those bloodless lips twisted in the agony of death. She had brushed back the beautiful strands of hair that fell in a soft mass on Celia's forehead. The face looked strangely different now that stark, white lids covered the sea-green eyes. Mona had tried to straighten the clenched hands but death had too strong a grip on them. From the corner of one fist trickled a few grains of yellow sand and dust long dead in the silent tomb. Dust, she thought, dust, old and new.

Her musings halted abruptly. A small object came flying through the air and fell into the farthest felucca. It must have come from one of the cabin windows below for Mona was close enough to see a small red box. She wondered what it could be. The thin metal or highly polished wood reflected the sun's rays. She thought for a moment that it might have fallen off a window ledge but soon dismissed that idea for it would have dropped straight down into the water instead of landing in the felucca. Anyway, the object was obviously thrown out, for it had come hurtling through the air.

But why was it thrown away? There were wastepaper baskets in each room and the Arab valet was always hovering around for any discarded object. Mona's interest was awakened. She ran quickly down to the lower deck and swinging over the rail stepped out into the first swaying little boat. Steadying herself against the side of the *dahabeah* she crawled over into the second bobbing craft. She could see the box plainly now but her arms were not quite long enough to reach it. The third boat was rocking dangerously on the little waves that the sudden motion had caused. It was with great difficulty that Mona clambered over its sides.

She picked up the box and to her surprise discovered it was a celluloid soap box. Made of thick material and red in color, it struck a familiar chord in Mona's memory. The top was gone and there was dirt ground in the grooves where it had screwed on. The bottom of the box was covered with half-dried mud and sand to which clung a few pieces of green grass and tiny bits of twigs.

It was certainly queer. Why should anyone deliberately throw away a soap box? And with such contents?

Suddenly Mona stood upright in the boat. It swayed perilously and with her left hand she gripped the mast to keep from falling. With her right she clung to the soap box.

Everything was clear now. No wonder it looked familiar. She had seen it on the shelf in Aunt Ella's bathroom. This was the missing box and it had recently contained not soap but a poisonous viper. That explained the dirt and grass.

But from what window had it been thrown? Mona turned her face toward the *dahabeah* and tried to figure out the right cabin. This was impossible though, for the bit of red celluloid might have come from any of them. She couldn't remember whether it had come straight or at an angle. Five cabins faced on this side of the boat. Amory had the one on the left end, Spencer the second one and Colonel and Mrs. Worthington the next two. Dr. Bradshaw occupied the cabin beneath the stairway on the right.

Just then the doctor appeared at his window and stared in surprise at the young girl. He started to ask a question, thought better of it and merely called out to her.

"Good morning, Mona. I am going to breakfast now with the others. Take care you don't fall." His words were a hidden warning.

"I'll be careful," said Mona, slipping the box into her pocket.

She climbed back to the *dahabeah* and went down to the dining-room. They were all there, even Sophie. Dr. Bradshaw sat by the door. He nodded his head to Mona who peered in cautiously. Now was the time to search the cabins.

CHAPTER XV
"THE END OF MY ROPE"

Mona turned the knob of Colonel Worthington's door. It opened just as she thought it would. People lock empty rooms against thieves, not murderers.

The cabin, which had not yet been cleaned by the substitute steward was, nevertheless, with the exception of a rumpled bed, tidy. Military brushes were placed neatly side by side on the dresser, pyjamas and dressing gown hung on a hook by the bed and even the sink was washed clean of all shaving soap and powder. She searched the dresser drawers, the wardrobe-trunk standing open by the wall, the bookshelves, and the writing desk. Everything seemed to be in perfect order. On the shelf above the sink was a yellow soap dish but there was nothing unusual about its contents.

The cabin rather vexed her, it was so neat, so utterly devoid of clues. She stood in the middle of the floor and looked about her. Not a false note. The room of an Englishman, orderly in his habits. Mona's eyes rested on a large box which lay on a little table by the bed. The word "chess" was stamped in a Florentine design on the leather top. That would be a good place to conceal a snake. She tried the lid and found it unlocked. Instead of containing large ivory chess men, as one would expect from the size of the box, it contained nothing but a slightly smaller leather box. This was locked and felt quite light. It was a jewel case.

What was it doing there? A jewel case concealed in a chess box. "I wonder," said Mona aloud and turned again to the desk. A great deal of correspondence was stacked in neat piles in the top drawer.

She glanced through it hurriedly. Bills, all bills, and some for large amounts, long past due.

The only false note. Colonel Worthington was fundamentally an orderly man. His room showed it. Yet his business was in a state of disorder. Bills, bills, bills. A man of well-regulated habits always pays his bills promptly unless he is in need of funds.

Perhaps he had killed Celia for money. But how would he profit by her death? Her property went to two cousins—the young school-girl and the newspaper man, John Stewart. What had Tom said about him? That Celia didn't like him and that he spent a great deal of time in India. So had Colonel Worthington. Maybe there was some connection.

Sophie's room came next. It was essentially feminine. The dressing table was covered with perfume bottles, powder boxes and various parts of a beautiful silver toilet-set. Exquisite lace underwear and what were evidently Sophie's night-things lay scattered about on the floor, on the chairs and the rumpled bed. The general impression was one of untidiness. It had the appearance of an actress's dressing-room. That's what it was, as a matter of fact. Mona wondered just how much acting Sophie had been doing lately. Certainly no particular love had existed between her and Celia, nor did she appear to be terribly grieved over the beautiful woman's death. Something in the past might be throwing its dark shadow over the boat now. Perhaps Sophie harbored a secret grudge against Celia for injuries inflicted back in New York five years ago. No one would know what they were except the two women, and Celia was silent forever. Of course, Sophie may have felt her husband was seeing too much of Celia and that Celia might tell him about his wife's past. Sophie's gay life as an actress, in all probability, contained unsavory chapters. Chapters which would be better for the Englishman not to know.

But if there were such episodes Mona found no confirmation of them in Sophie's room. Her correspondence was of a trifling nature—a few notes from Paris dressmakers, several bills, a letter from a London banker dealing with the sale of some bank stock and a short, apparently harmless, cablegram which read "Planning on seeing you in Paris next month S."

Nothing else of interest presented itself in Sophie's room. If she had concealed the snake or was still concealing one there was no sign of it. Mona looked through every box and bag to no purpose. Sophie's silver and crystal soap box lay in clear view on the sink. It matched the rest of her toilet set and appeared to be serving its function as a container for soap, not poisonous snakes.

Glancing at her watch, she found ten minutes of her precious time gone. With an exclamation Mona started for the door. Her foot struck something hard which on examination proved to be a little black screw about half an inch long. Feeling about on the floor she discovered another screw even smaller. Little black screws. What did they mean? But this wasn't the time to stop and think. She must hurry.

Jack Spencer's room was almost as tidy as Colonel Worthington's. Two letters in his handsome writing case attracted her attention. They were post-marked "St. Jean de Luz." Mona remembered hearing of the town. It was a fashionable resort in the Basque Country containing many gambling establishments. She put the letters in her pocket until later. It would be safer to read them in her cabin.

With a feeling akin to disappointment Mona turned to leave the room when her eyes fell on the closet. The door was slightly open. She searched the shelves and floor but found nothing unusual. As she straightened up from her stooped position her shoulder brushed against a pair of white trousers, knocking them off the hook. She picked them up and noticed across the knees two black streaks. Grease. The engine room was the only place on the *dahabeah* where Jack Spencer could have run into so much axle grease. She remembered the trousers. He had worn them yesterday, the day of the murders.

Mona shrugged her shoulders. What could grease have to do with murder?

Tom's room was next. Mona found no clues in any of the dresser drawers or luggage scattered about. It was not until she reached the waste-paper basket. Here her search stopped for it contained three unfinished notes addressed to Celia and dated the night before she was murdered. There were only a few lines on each note. Evidently Tom had found difficulty in expressing what he wanted to say.

All the notes were more or less alike. Mona picked one out of the lot. It read: "I have come to the end of my rope. Beginning with tomorrow things will be different. Charlie Worthington—"

"I would like to see the finished note," said Mona softly. "And I think I know where it is."

CHAPTER XVI
THE MISSING KEY

"And so," Mona concluded, "that's as far as I got. I wasn't able to search the other cabins for just as I left Tom's room the boat struck a mud bank and I knew you couldn't hold the passengers in the dining salon any longer."

"They rushed from the room in a body," said Dr. Bradshaw, leaning back in his swivel chair. "It was unfortunate we hit shallow water just then. I wonder what you would have found in Professor Cross's room?"

"Nothing, I'm sure," Mona was emphatic. "Professor Cross is too clever a man to leave clews about that an amateur like me would find."

"He is a cool, analytical sort of person," agreed the doctor. Little rings of perspiration were gathering under his eyes and his white collar was limp.

"You look tired," said Mona suddenly. This fat little man was strangely pathetic at times.

"I am. I have never been so worried in all my life. You see," he spread out his pudgy hands wearily, "I shall lose my job—even if I get back to Assuan alive."

"It's not your fault. How could you help it?"

"I couldn't. But all these terrible things have happened—and perhaps are still happening—on my *dahabeah*. The Company will blame me."

"If we find the murderer before we reach Assuan they won't blame you."

"But can we? I have the feeling we're just skimming the surface. I sat at breakfast with seven people. One of them was a criminal, or an absolute maniac, yet I couldn't have put my finger on him to save my life. I tell you, it's hopeless."

Mona made no comment but fingered the bruised spots on her neck gingerly. "I hunted for you after breakfast, Doctor," she said after a moment's silence, "but you were nowhere to be found."

"If there's one thing the Arab sailors know, it is how to shove a boat off a mud bank. My crew have forgotten even that. They are so panic-stricken from Abdu's murder they are a lot of helpless dummies. I have been down in the hull for a solid hour directing them to do something that they could do far better alone—provided this were an ordinary steamer and not a floating horror." Dr. Bradshaw fumbled for his tobacco pouch abstractedly. The little brown flakes stuck to his wet fingers as he stuffed his pipe. With the lighted match in his hand, he looked up at Mona.

"Was there anything you especially wanted with me?"

"Yes, the key to Celia's room. I'm sure Tom's finished note is in there somewhere. I believe that note will tell us a lot about the murder. And I'm anxious to get my hands on it before the idea occurs to Tom. When I couldn't find you, I decided to get in without a key."

"Without a key?" Dr. Bradshaw was surprised. "How could you do that?"

"Through the empty room of the suite Celia occupied. A bath, you know, separates rooms 7A and 7B."

"Still I don't see," Dr. Bradshaw shook his head uncomprehendingly. "The door was locked between the bath and the empty room."

"I found that out," said. Mona. "I admit I was stumped for a moment. Then I thought of Jimmie. He's quite an athlete and it occurred to me that he might get in by climbing through the transom. I felt I could trust Jimmie and it would be much easier for him to climb through than for me with my skirts. So I asked him to do it as a special favor. At first he said 'no' but after I told him I'd try it myself, skirts or no skirts, he agreed. As I finished talking to him Jack Spencer strolled up and I suppose he had to get rid of him first."

"Let's go down for it ourselves," suggested the doctor.

Mona hesitated before she spoke.

"I don't think we'd better," she said finally. "Jimmie might be in there and if we suddenly unlocked the door it would scare him to death. Let's wait until he comes up."

"Just as you say. I don't envy him his job though. I'd never get through a transom on a hot day like this." He wriggled his body uncomfortably beneath linen that had lost its freshness.

"Jimmie is probably the only one who could except, perhaps, Professor Cross. That man is thin enough to go through a keyhole."

Dr. Bradshaw removed the pipe from his rather weak lips.

"Professor Cross? He said a peculiar thing at breakfast. I was sitting at the table between him and Miss Singlefoot. She had been doing most of the talking when suddenly he dropped his fork and asked her a question that I thought was queer."

"Queer?" Mona was interested.

"Yes, queer. Miss Singlefoot was saying that they never cooked her eggs enough and for no rhyme or reason, as far as I could see, he said, 'You remember the Haines murder, I suppose?' She didn't understand and sat there repeating aloud, 'The Haines murder?' in a blank voice. Then Professor Cross stood up and leaned across the table toward her. 'Old Mrs. Haines,' he said, 'was a moral, religious fanatic. She killed her two nieces because they were not good women.' He stood for a moment staring at your aunt and then turned and walked out of the dining-room. What do you think he meant by that? What was the Haines murder? Was it something that happened in America?"

"Yes, it was headlines in all the papers a few years ago. I was a cub reporter at the time and I remember it distinctly. Mrs. Haines, who was afterwards found to be insane, poisoned her two nieces. They lived with her in an apartment in New York. She had gotten the idea that they were immoral, as they probably were, and for that reason took it upon herself to punish them. But what made him ask Aunt Ella about it? I don't understand."

"Neither do I."

"Professor Cross frightens me," said Mona. "When he looks at me I feel a cold chill run up my spine. He's all brain and no heart. If he had a grudge against a person I believe he'd wipe him out without a qualm. I frankly admit I'll be glad to see the last of him."

There was a sharp knock at the door.

"Come in," said Dr. Bradshaw rising from his chair with an effort.

The door opened and Professor Cross stood on the threshold.

"Am I interrupting a conference?" he asked, resting his cold eyes first on the doctor and then questioningly on Mona.

"Not at all. Have a seat." Dr. Bradshaw indicated a chair and offered the man a cigarette. "I keep them for callers," he explained. "I smoke a pipe myself."

"I never smoke anything," said Professor Cross in a negative voice. "I consider all use of tobacco a bad habit." He glanced disapprovingly at Mona, who was smoking.

No one spoke for a minute. Dr. Bradshaw's chair squeaked exasperatingly beneath his weight.

"The other passengers are very nervous this morning," remarked Professor Cross. "If we don't get out of this hot hole soon I believe something terrible will happen from pure hysteria. When do you think we'll reach Assuan?"

The doctor was wreathed in a cloud of smoke. He puffed at his pipe noisily.

"Tonight with good luck. More likely tomorrow morning early."

"It would be well if we got there this evening. I don't think we can stand another night of suspense."

"The Arabs may desert at any moment," said the doctor pessimistically. "And if they do I don't know when we'll reach civilization. It would depend on how you and the rest of the men helped me push through."

"I have never done manual labor." Professor Cross held up his hands. "My fingers have no strength in them."

Mona stared at his fingers. They were long and thin. Was he telling the truth? Was he the watcher in the dark who had choked her with a vise-like grip? She shuddered involuntarily. Somehow, she felt weak in the presence of this man.

"Have you made any progress in your investigations, Doctor?" he asked through thin lips.

"Some," Dr. Bradshaw was almost abrupt.

"Have you searched the cabins?" continued Professor Cross in an unruffled voice.

"They've been searched," was the non-committal reply.

"I have been thinking that if I were doing the investigating I'd hunt for a pair of thick leather gloves." There was a slight emphasis on the word "leather."

"Why gloves?" asked the doctor in a puzzled voice.

"One doesn't handle an asp without them. Find the person who owns a pair of thick leather gloves and you'll have the one who put the asp in Miss Lawton's pocket."

Mona stared at the Professor, fascinated. Why hadn't she thought of that? Gloves, soap containers. Was there a connection?

"But if one wore kid gloves in Africa, even in the early morning, we'd all notice it," Dr. Bradshaw reminded them. "I believe the viper was put in Miss Lawton's pocket after we left for the tombs yesterday. Therefore, the murderer couldn't have worn such gloves for it would have been a dead give-away."

"The murderer wore kid gloves," repeated Professor Cross in the tone one uses to explain something to a child. "Moreover, we don't know that the asp was put in the coat pocket early yesterday morning. It might have been put there the night before for it probably wouldn't have stirred from its hiding place. These African vipers love heat and unless they are disturbed, they never move from a warm spot. A camel's hair pocket would be warm and comfortable. There is no doubt," he concluded, "that the murderer wore leather gloves."

A thoroughly disagreeable man, thought Mona. Conceited and narrow-minded. But in one way he was right. No one would handle an asp without heavy gloves. Yet, on the other hand, if one wore leather gloves in Africa there would be comment and a murderer couldn't risk that. From this reasoning one conclusion seemed obvious; the asp must have been concealed in the pocket during the night or early in the morning when Celia was at breakfast.

Professor Cross was talking again.

"Do you remember asking Miss Singlefoot if she heard anything in the corridor the night before the murder?"

"I asked her that question and she denied hearing anything," said the doctor shortly. He didn't like this intellectually arrogant man.

"She hesitated before she spoke," returned the author. "I believe she heard something or someone. The murderer perhaps."

A fly buzzed noisily against the ceiling. The heat came in waves through the window. Mona wished for some ice water and then remembered wearily there was none.

"Yes," repeated Professor Cross, rising from his chair unhurriedly. "I would find out the identity of Miss Lawton's night visitor. Then you'll have the murderer. At least, you'll know who he is. They are two different things."

He walked to the door with barely a glance in Mona's direction. Dr. Bradshaw followed him.

"If I can help you in your investigations, Doctor, please call on me. I am interested from a scientific point of view. Analytical problems are always a pleasure."

Professor Cross closed the door quietly. Dr. Bradshaw walked to the window and stared out toward the hot, still sands of the Sahara. The monotonous churning of the paddle-wheel shook the stuffy little room.

"Come!" Mona got up from her chair suddenly. "Let's go down to Celia's room. I have a feeling something's wrong. Jimmie's been gone too long."

"All right," said the doctor, taking a key-ring from his desk drawer. He ran his fingers hurriedly over the keys. A dull red flush stained his face. Little heads of perspiration popped out on his forehead and rolled down his nose. He stared at the keys in his hand.

"The key to Celia's room is missing," he said.

CHAPTER XVII
THE MAN IN THE DEATH CHAMBER

They met Jimmie in the corridor. His face was chalky white and his eyes were those of a man haunted by a terrible apparition. He tried to speak, but his lips moved noiselessly.

"What's the matter, boy?" asked the doctor, gripping his shoulder.

"What have you been doing so long?" Mona felt a heavy hand enclosing her heart and smothering it.

Jimmie stared at her dully. Through blue lips came the words, "I have been locked in the bathroom watching the murderer."

"Come into my office, quick!" Dr. Bradshaw looked back over his shoulder. If the murderer listened behind any of those closed doors, Jimmie Bean's life was not worth tuppence.

"I'll never forgive myself for sending you on such an errand," said Mona, hovering on the arm of his chair. "Tell us, did you get the letter?"

"No, I didn't get the letter but someone else did."

"You saw the murderer? Who was it?" Perspiration streamed down the doctor's face. His words came in nervous little jerks.

"I don't know. I watched him through the keyhole of the bathroom door. I couldn't see his face."

Jimmie was gradually getting back his composure. He took a handkerchief from his pocket and wiped the palms of his hands. He looked at Mona with a crooked little smile.

"Lord, but I was scared. I stood behind that door like a frozen image. I could see Celia's distorted lips, Abdu's staring eyes, and I could feel those awful choking hands. I swear, I was in a cold sweat."

"Swallow this down and tell us about it." Dr. Bradshaw handed him a brimming whiskey glass. Mona noticed with surprise that the doctor's hands were shaking like one suffering from palsy.

"To begin with," said Jimmie slowly, "when I got in Room 7A, the empty one of Celia's suite, I shut the hall door carefully after making sure no one saw me enter. Then I tried the little metal lever that operates the transom above the bathroom door but it was broken. So I climbed up on the wardrobe and gave the edge of the transom a push. It didn't budge. I tried again and the frame moved a little. After a couple of pushes I got it all the way open and then crawled through. I slid down into the bathtub, and darned if it didn't have some water in it." Jimmie pointed to his tan and white sport shoes, the white of which had now become a dingy yellow.

"From that time on," he continued, "there was plenty of trouble. Just as I turned the knob of the door I heard a key being inserted in a lock. I let go of the knob quickly and waited, leaning against the panel. Then I heard the door that leads into Celia's room from the corridor being quietly opened, closed and locked again. Someone was in that room with the dead body. I stooped to peer through the keyhole. I figured if it were the doctor, it was all right, but if it weren't it was the murderer and I was in a terrible jam. I could see to the waist of a man dressed in a white suit, a tall man. It could not have been the doctor. It was someone who had no business in the room—someone who was trying to be very quiet—someone who was listening for noises. I could see him move a little distance and then stop to see if he was overheard. The horrible realization came over me that if he should open the bathroom door I couldn't escape. I was like a rabbit caught in a trap. My heart was in my throat and I felt my knees giving way under me. I had to press the back of my hand against my mouth to keep from shouting bloody murder."

Jimmie paused for a moment and stirred nervously in his chair at the memory.

"The man was moving about. I could hear him breathing—quick, deep breaths. He had stepped out of my line of vision. A drawer squeaked. I think it was the desk drawer. There was a queer little shuffling noise as if he were going through some papers. The sound stopped and I heard the word 'good' in a low, satisfied voice. There was another silence and then came a sharp rip of paper being torn. A match was struck against a hard surface and I smelled paper burning. This took a long time, or so it seemed to me leaning against that sticky wood. I tell you, the blood was pounding in my temples like it does when I've been running hard."

"Go on," urged Mona, "what happened next?"

"The man was moving again. I could see his legs going toward the bed. I could get a glimpse of the head of the bed and something hidden beneath a white sheet. Only one leg was now in my line of vision. I saw the sheet ripple. He had uncovered part of the body. I couldn't see what he was doing, though he stood still a long time. There wasn't a sound except his harsh breathing. It was horrible, getting only a narrow strip of the whole picture. My imagination filled in the missing parts. I had the feeling I was choking. If I could only have gotten out of that stuffy little bathroom. But there was no chance of squeezing through the transom without being heard. Before I could have been half through, that unknown man would have pulled me back.

"Suddenly the sheet rippled again. He was covering the body. He moved to the door and hesitated a second. I was breathing so loud I was sure he had heard me. An eternity passed. Then the key turned in the lock and he was gone. I waited one long minute by my watch before I moved. Then I crawled through the transom and came up here. I'm all shot," he concluded weakly, fumbling for his cigarettes.

Mona silently handed him a lighted match, and watched him puff great clouds of smoke into the hot air.

"That was Tom," she said, "after the letter. But what was he doing bending over Celia's body? Was he removing some evidence that Dr. Bradshaw had failed to see?"

"Somehow," Jimmie's words were thoughtful, "those legs didn't look like they belonged to Tom. Nor did the steps sound like Tom's. They were short and springy. Like—" Jimmie hesitated for a moment, then finished with conviction—"like Colonel Worthington's."

Mona's mind raced back to an orderly room with a pile of unpaid bills—to an unfinished note with its tantalizing last words, "Charlie Worthington." What was on the burned piece that someone feared?

CHAPTER XVIII
GATHERING CLOUDS

"Did Tom Amory tell you what happened last night?" Jimmie turned to Dr. Bradshaw, who shook his head at the question.

"No," he said, "what was it?"

"Someone tried to enter his cabin. He got up to investigate and he swears he heard the sound of a chuckle outside his door. Of course, he hasn't any more of a gun than the rest of us, so he was careful how he went out into the dark hall."

The doctor's voice contained a puzzled note as he continued. "Dark hall? The lights were on when I went to my cabin. I checked up on them."

Jimmie was thinking that the doctor alone had a gun. He was the only one on the boat who had.

"Tom says the circuit was cut. After he heard his lock turning he put on his bathrobe, took a lighted candle and traipsed up and down the hall. He knocked on Jack's door first and then on Colonel Worthington's. Jack refused to open his door. The Colonel opened his immediately and stood there talking to him. What do you reckon the murderer wanted in Tom's room?"

"Did Spencer or Colonel Worthington hear anything?" Mona was watching Dr. Bradshaw out of the corner of her eye.

"Nothing except the noise that Tom made in his investigating."

"Maybe that was all the noise there was," said Mona thoughtfully.

"What do you mean?" asked Jimmie in surprise.

"Simply this. Perhaps Tom has his own reason for wanting us to think someone was prowling around during the night. This story of his might be a fairy tale invented to cover any noises or slips that

may have been made on his part. After all, who could be a more logical candidate for the murderer than the rejected lover? I'd take a bet
it was Tom you saw in Celia's room and I know what he was after."

"The murderer," said Dr. Bradshaw slowly, "has shown himself
to be a versatile fellow. He kills twice in a most thorough and different way. The weapon of death in both instances completely dis-
appears. He strangles Miss Case in the dark, perhaps as a warning
to beware of interfering, or perhaps as an intended death. He stops
at nothing. Blackmail, therefore, would not be out of the question.
He may have slipped in Celia's room and stolen the note that damns
Mr. Amory."

"But the note was destroyed," protested Jimmie.

"You didn't see him destroy it—you merely think he did. He
might have been burning some other piece of paper. Perhaps Amory
wrote a second note apologizing for the first. That first note, in the
light of Celia's death, would be a powerful weapon in the hands of
the murderer. Amory, as the likely suspect, couldn't risk the chance
of its being brought to the front. The murderer, knowing this, may
have wanted the note for blackmail. There may be still another reason. If the guilty man should get in a tight place, that note could be
used to divert suspicion. I'll wager it was stolen either for blackmail
or as a defense mechanism."

Conviction was in the fat little doctor's manner. His eyes gleamed
behind damp lenses. They were prominent eyes, looming large in his
red face.

"You don't think, then, that Tom and the murderer are one person?" said Mona quietly.

"No, I do not."

"I wonder what was going on last night? Must have been something or else the lights wouldn't have been cut off." Jimmie rose to
his feet and stared out of the porthole. The land was becoming less
flat, bleak sand dunes were appearing along the water's edge. Deso-
lation, dull and despairing, was closing in upon the little boat.

Dr. Bradshaw stepped to the door and poked out his head. "Seraf," he called twice, his words echoing back to the two in the office.
Mona wondered vaguely why he hadn't rung the electric bell and
then remembered the current was not on.

The shuffling of carpeted feet was heard in the corridor. Seraf, the deck steward, his black face shriveled and weather-beaten, appeared in the doorway.

"You call, sir?" he asked, his dark eyes roving about the room.

"Yes, I did. Go down to Miss Davet's room and tell her to come to my office."

"Yes, sir." He shuffled off in the opposite direction from which he had come.

No one said a word. They waited silently for the arrival of Miss Lawton's personal maid.

It is curious that up to this moment no one had thought of Jane Davet either as a suspect herself or as one who might be of great help in finding the murderer. In the excitement she had been overlooked entirely. Such is the inconsistency of amateur detectives.

In a very short time the Englishwoman appeared. She was of slight stature, dark and homely. Mona was surprised to see on each of her prominent cheek-bones an irregular dab of rouge. It was clear that make-up was new to Jane. Why the sudden desire for beautification?

"You will go with me, Jane," said the doctor rising from his chair and shaking down his trouser leg, "to Miss Lawton's room. I want to pack her things."

"To Miss Lawton's room?" Terror was written on the woman's plain face. "Oh, no, sir," she said, "I couldn't."

"Why not?" Dr. Bradshaw was irritated.

"I'm afraid, sir. I don't like the dead."

"Tommyrot," he snorted disgustedly. "No one asked you to have anything to do with the corpse. You are to pack Miss Lawton's belongings, that's all. I want to see if everything is intact. Do you understand?"

"Yes, sir. I'll go, sir." She kept clasping and unclasping her hands—thick hands of the low-class English servant. A queer maid for Celia, thought Mona. A sophisticated French mademoiselle would have been the more likely type.

"I'll see you all later," said the doctor, following Jane out into the corridor. "Meanwhile, don't wander off alone. You're safe only in groups."

"You'd better be careful, too," said Mona impulsively.

Dr. Bradshaw pulled a revolver halfway out of his hip pocket.

"I am careful," he answered grimly and disappeared from sight.

Mona and Jimmie stared at each other.

"He has a gun and someone is hiding the second poisonous viper. I'm afraid, terribly afraid."

"We all are," Jimmie reminded her. "We're afraid of each other."

They left the close little office and went out on deck. The air was thick and heavy and a dark speck in the sky hung over the horizon of the Sahara Desert.

"Curious, that dark cloud," remarked Jimmie, speculation in his voice.

"Clouds always gather before storms," said Mona listlessly.

CHAPTER XIX
PEBBLES FOR STONES

Dr. Bradshaw sat in the middle of the room and watched Jane Davet pack. She didn't do it well—her movements were clumsy and uncertain. The look in her eyes closely resembled fear. But that was to be expected. The uneducated English are superstitious and, almost without exception, skittish in the presence of the dead.

He had examined the body for the third time. No change in its condition was noticeable other than the decomposition expected in such heat. If the unknown intruder of the dead had handled the body there was no evidence of it. The corpse was as the doctor had last seen it—a bit of clay from which all physical and spiritual beauty had fled.

He sat fidgeting in his chair. The room was hot—oppressively so. A dread odor pervaded it, enveloping the two human beings in a cloud as ominous as it was cloying. The journey must end soon or else—

Dr. Bradshaw pulled himself together with a jerk. He would get to Assuan that night, by God, even if he had to steam up the boat himself. That still, dead form under the white sheet was a menace to the living. The atmosphere of the room seemed to shriek at him a warning that unless they got off the boat before the morrow, something else would happen.

He glanced at his watch. Why didn't Jane hurry?

Twenty minutes had gone. What was she doing now? Strange, the way she stared into the top drawer.

"What's the matter?" he asked. "Anything wrong?"

He could see her reflection in the mirror. There was a tautness to her figure, a stunned expression in her dark eyes.

"Miss Lawton's jewel case is gone. It was here in the top drawer. But it's gone now."

"Are you sure?" he asked, only slightly alarmed. "Couldn't it be in some other place?"

"I have looked in all the other places. I tell you, sir, it's not here. It's gone, gone."

Dr. Bradshaw's face showed his surprise. The maid had become terribly agitated. Her voice was shrill and she avoided his gaze. Her head kept turning to the door, like a nervous animal caught at bay. Did she fear someone's approach or was she simply anxious to get away from this chamber of death?

"What do you mean by 'gone'? It's been stolen." His voice was stern and the woman seemed to become more terrified.

"Not stolen, sir. No one would dare steal from a dead person." She was stuttering in her fright.

"It's been done," said the doctor grimly. "Besides, someone dared murder your mistress. That same person would not hesitate to commit a theft."

He paused for a second and stared down into the empty drawer. Then he closed it with a bang, and shoved the frightened woman toward the door.

"Come along with me," he said. "We haven't time to stand here gaping at nothing. I'll want to ask you some questions."

"But I don't know anything about it, sir. I don't know anything, sir." Her voice ended in a sob. "Oh, let's get out of this awful room."

They were in the corridor and the doctor had locked the door. Mona Case was standing in front of Miss Singlefoot's cabin with her hand on the door-knob.

"Miss Case," called the doctor, "will you come to my office for a moment? I have something to tell you." His words were heavy with meaning.

Mona started to ask a question, but an ever-present instinct cautioned her to wait. She fell in step without a word, her thoughts racing.

Dr. Bradshaw closed his office door and stood facing the two women in the dim light of the little room. They did not think to question the absence of bright sunlight. Their weary bodies accepted without question the relief of clouded skies.

"Miss Lawton's jewel case has been stolen." His voice was flat.

"Stolen! When?" gasped Mona in the same breath.

"I don't know," replied the doctor. "Perhaps in the night when the lights were off. Mr. Amory probably told the truth, after all."

He turned to the maid. "When was the last time you saw the jewelry box?"

Evidently she was struggling to collect her thoughts. "Now, let me see, sir. Sometime the day before yesterday; I don't remember when."

"But you must," said the doctor sternly. "Think hard. It is very important."

Jane Davet was silent for a moment. Deep perplexity was written on her tense face.

"I remember now," she said slowly, as if feeling for her words. "It was while I was dressing Miss Lawton's hair for dinner. I opened the drawer for some fresh hairpins. I saw the jewel box and I said, 'What jewels tonight, Miss?' and she said, 'None at all, Jane.'"

"How long did you stay in her cabin after she left for dinner?"

"About half an hour."

"What did you do during that time?"

"I straightened the cabin and laid out Miss Lawton's night things."

"Did you go back to the room later in the evening?"

"No, I was through for the night. I was always free after eight o'clock. Miss Lawton did not require me when she went to bed. She liked to be alone." Jane glanced meaningly at the doctor, who ignored the look. "Was Miss Lawton an easy person to work for?" he continued.

"Yes, she was. She was always kind to me." There was a marked restraint in her tone.

"Do you have any suspicions regarding the missing jewels?"

"No, sir," the answer came readily. Too readily for the agitation she had shown in the dead woman's cabin.

"Are you sure you are keeping nothing from me?"

His voice was harsh. It did not move Jane to an explanation, though, for she was growing more and more reticent.

"I have told you all I know," she said.

"Dr. Bradshaw," put in Mona suddenly, "may I ask a question?"

"Certainly. Go right ahead."

"What sort of a case was it, Jane? Describe it, please."

"It was of rose-colored Florentine leather. Not so very large, Miss." The woman seemed much surer of herself in this room that was empty of the dead.

"Did the case contain many valuable jewels?" continued Mona.

Jane Davet hesitated.

"Speak up," snapped the doctor in a voice frayed with nervousness.

"I think so, sir."

"Think so—don't you know?" He glared at her.

"Yes, sir. I mean, I believe so, sir."

"Hell," said the doctor.

But Mona wasn't listening. She was thinking of a very neat cabin and of a chess box.

"I know where that case is," she said slowly. "I'll be back in a minute."

And she was, the jewel case under her arm.

"Where did you find it?" asked the doctor, taking it in his hands.

"In Colonel Worthington's cabin, concealed in a chess box."

"You'd better be careful, young lady, how you go bursting into people's cabins. It's dangerous business."

"I know," said Mona soberly. "I made sure the Colonel was upstairs before I went near his room. Even then I knocked first."

She was watching Jane's face. The little red rouge spots fascinated her. They were the only bit of color in a dark face that was strangely sallow.

"It is locked," remarked the doctor, trying the lid, "and not very heavy."

He shook the box. A gleam of satisfaction came into his eyes. "But it is not empty. Listen to the jewels." He shook the box again. "An expensive noise," he concluded, irrelevantly.

"Let's open it," suggested Mona, still staring at Jane. Why should the maid be so nervous, so ill at ease?

Dr. Bradshaw took a small penknife from his pocket.

"I'll pry it open," he explained.

The two women watched his movements in silence. The man's breath came in little gasps. The knife's blade was not strong enough. He flung it on the desk in disgust. For a second he peered about uncertainly.

"This will do it," he muttered and picked up a slender letter opener. The metal was hard and unyielding. Under its pressure the lock gave immediately and the doctor stared down into the contents of the case. All satisfaction seemed to leave him. His body wilted.

"Well, I'll be damned," he sputtered and held the box out to Mona.

She found herself looking down into a tray filled with small white pebbles.

"Pebbles for stones," she said, lifting her eyes to Jane Davet's face. She saw no surprise there, only fear. Fear of something, sure and unrelenting.

CHAPTER XX
RIVERS OF SAND

The dark speck in the sky that Mona and Jimmie had seen was no longer something distant. It had been the silent announcer of a sandstorm which now swept the Sahara Desert and the little boat with its heat-weary, death-tortured cargo. The hot wind from the inland was bowing all before it and in its arms it carried great burdens of sand, yellow, blinding sand. It encompassed the little wooden craft and penetrated its very depths. Sand trickled in at the windows and doors, invading the boat's interior in live little streams, crooked and yellow.

The sailors had been compelled to tie up on the bank. It was a hard job, for the *dahabeah* careened wildly beneath the force of the wind. It came perilously near to tipping over several times. The generally placid and sluggish water of the Nile was tossing great waves against its sides. All the forces of nature seemed to be plotting against this one lone boat, so helpless and so full of fear.

The passengers were in an uproar. With the exception of Miss Singlefoot and Dr. Bradshaw they were congregated in the card room. They were miserable and misery loves company, be it congenial or otherwise. Moreover, when together, they forgot the growing fear that seized each one alone. But they could not forget their irritation and jumpy nerves. The electricity was still out of commission and flickering candlelight made card playing and chess difficult. The conversation was disjointed. On only one topic did the group agree and that topic was that the situation was bad. Moreover, it was steadily growing worse. If the storm kept up, there was little hope of reaching Assuan by night.

"I wish to God I had a drink," said Jack Spencer, his eyes fixed moodily on a little pile of sand just inside the door.

"Why don't you get one," suggested Professor Cross. "If you wait for the Arabs to bring it, you'll have a long wait. They are too busy keeping the ship afloat in this storm to fetch you whiskey. You must remember that it was Abdu who formerly supplied you with the necessary drinks. He's dead now." Professor Cross laughed maliciously. "That's a good one," he cackled, "on the murderer. No one to bring him his drinks." He continued to laugh, almost noiselessly, and to mutter under his breath, "a good one."

"I think sardonic humor is out of place in this situation," remarked Jack Spencer finally. "But, at that, I'm going to take your advice. I'll go myself." He closed the door and went out on the sand-beaten deck.

"He's getting to be a cordial cuss—not," muttered Colonel Worthington. "He might have had the decency to offer to bring some of the rest of us a drink. Selfish ass."

"Why not go with him?" suggested Sophie, with a hint of sarcasm in her voice.

"You know damn well why I don't," retorted her husband. "You won't catch me going anywhere with a single person on this boat. I don't trust any of them." He glared suspiciously around the room. "And if you listen to me, you won't either. There's no telling what will happen in such a storm. Why, out on deck you can't see your hand before you. A nice place for a murder. Phew!" He took a handkerchief from his pocket and wiped his forehead. "Even sand on my face. We'll be eating it next."

"I don't see why the electrician on this tub doesn't fix the lights," remarked Jimmie.

"Electrician!" scoffed Professor Cross. "The *Assuit* doesn't possess one. Dr. Bradshaw is the only person who knows anything about electricity and he can't find the cause of the trouble.

"By the way, Mr. Amory," said Sophie, "I understand you are an engineer. Not an electrical one, I suppose.

"No, civil," answered Tom briefly.

"It's a pity," returned Sophie and lapsed into silence. Her face relaxed for a moment and Mona noticed the tired little lines about her eyes and mouth. Everyone was showing the strain and someone would be the first to snap under it. Who would it be?

Mona started for the door.

"Where are you going?" asked Jimmie.

"Down to Aunt Ella's room to see what's keeping her. I'll be back in a minute."

She was gone and Jimmie made a move as if to follow.

"Better stay here," advised Sophie. "I think Charlie is right. Crowds are safer."

Jimmie glanced at her sharply. An exasperating woman. How like her to suggest the possibility of Mona's being afraid of him. And as for his being afraid of Mona—bosh! He wished he had gone with her. But it was too late. No doubt she was already in Miss Singlefoot's room.

And he was right. By this time Mona had fought her way through the sand and wind and had reached the dark corridor of the lower deck. She knocked on her aunt's door but no sound came from within. She knocked again, more loudly this time, but only the shriek of the wind answered her. She opened the door and peered into the room. An amazing sight met her eyes. Miss Singlefoot was crouched at the foot of the bed with her left ear glued to the lower window casement. Her body was rigid and she did not appear to notice her niece.

"What in the world?" gasped Mona.

"Sh-sh-sh," hissed Miss Singlefoot, her fingers to her lips. "Come here."

Mona closed the door softly and started across the floor. Just as she reached the window Miss Singlefoot arose from her stooped position.

"Shucks," she said in disgust. "They must have heard you come in."

"Will you please tell me what's going on, Aunt Ella?"

"Plenty," snapped that tall and angular person.

"Who heard me coming?" insisted Mona. "And where were they?"

"That low-life Jack Spencer and that sneaking English maid. They were outside my window in the corner where the next room juts out."

"How do you know? You couldn't see them."

"Of course not, but I could hear them." Then she added in a withering tone, "That is, until you came blundering in."

"Tell me about it," suggested Mona, settling herself in an uncomfortable straight chair.

"Well, I was lying there in bed when I heard a sound like someone walking on the deck outside my cabin and then low voices. I didn't pay much attention at first, but I couldn't help hearing parts of a conversation. Two people were standing just outside my cabin. The bottom edge of the window is a bit warped and noises drift in. Suddenly I heard the word 'police.' Then I began to take notice. I crawled out of bed and put my ear to the window where the sounds were loudest. I couldn't make out everything that was said for they were talking low and not very distinctly. I got the general drift, though. Jane kept saying something about turning him over to the police if he were lying. I heard him remonstrate with her and use the word 'gambling.' He repeated several times, 'I had to do it to pay a debt.' Then he said something about getting into someone's confidence. I wasn't able to make all that out. You came in about that time and they moved away."

"I'm shocked," said Mona.

"I'm not," retorted her aunt. "There's been a lot of crooked things going on around here that no one seems to notice."

"Just for instance?" urged Mona, sitting forward in her chair.

"Well, Mr. Spencer has been extremely friendly with this Jane person. He's been meeting her on the sly."

"Why didn't you tell me this before?"

"Never thought of it, to tell the truth. All the excitement drove it out of my mind. It was two nights ago that I first saw them together. I was taking a walk around the deck and when I got to that dark corner between the stern and the back stairs I heard someone talking in a low tone. I stood still and listened. About a minute later a door opened somewhere on the deck below and a shaft of light fell across their faces. I saw it was Mr. Spencer and Jane."

"It may mean anything, Aunt Ella. Perhaps Jane was delivering a message to him from Celia. It's likely."

"Likely!" Miss Singlefoot was thoroughly indignant. "Well, maybe, but that's not what happened. Do you know what I saw when the light fell on the pair?"

"I haven't the slightest idea."

"He had his arms around her and she was smoothing down his hair with both of her hands." Miss Singlefoot sat back in triumph to watch the effect on Mona.

"Fastidious Jack Spencer playing around with an ordinary maid," exclaimed Mona disgustedly. "Now I wonder what connection he has with Jane? Is he by any chance in love with her or is there some other reason?"

"I don't believe he loves anyone but himself," retorted Miss Singlefoot. "No doubt the two of them got together and murdered Celia and stole the jewels. Jane probably hated her mistress. She looks like the kind to harbor a grudge. As for Mr. Spencer, well, the least I can say is that I'm disappointed in him. He's not the man I thought he was."

"Aunt Ella," said Mona slowly, looking at Miss Singlefoot with a speculative light in her eye, "what about Professor Cross? Do you think he might have killed Celia, and later, Abdu?"

"Mona Case, are you crazy? Professor Cross is the nicest man I ever saw. What would he be running around killing people for? Besides, where's his motive? You don't kill people without a motive, and he hasn't one."

"Somehow I can't get over seeing that gleam in his eyes the night before Celia was murdered."

"What gleam?" snorted Miss Singlefoot. "And what does a silly little gleam have to do with murder?"

"I admit that Celia never showed any particular dislike for Professor Cross. She was merely indifferent and bored with his blatant erudition. But Professor Cross was annoyed with her the night before she died when she laughed so openly at his talk about the temples and tombs. A scholar is a very sensitive person and any slighting of his knowledge is magnified by him to large proportions."

"You may be right," sniffed Miss Singlefoot in an unconvinced tone. "But I don't think Professor Cross was hurt enough to do murder for it. He's such a gentle soul."

Mona sighed wearily. From experience she knew it was hopeless to argue with her aunt.

"Incidentally, Mona, what about Jimmie Bean? Wasn't he a bit friendly with Celia, too?"

"Of course, Jimmie was friendly with Celia. We all were, more or less. But it's ridiculous to suspect him. He's just a kid."

"Well, plenty of boys have fallen in love with older women. It happens every day. I read it in the paper and I know it for a fact. Celia may have turned him down and then he decided if he couldn't have her, no one else would."

"Be reasonable. What does he know about poisonous vipers? He's never lived in the Orient."

"He may know more than he's telling. Don't think because he's young he couldn't have done it. Murderers are growing younger every day. Why, I read in *Sawyer's Center Weekly* about a boy, fourteen years old, killing his school teacher with an axe."

"All the same," returned Mona, "I think it's foolish to consider Jimmie."

"Have it your own way," said Miss Singlefoot, closing her lips primly. "I don't agree, though. Young people are not what they used to be. They'd all bear watching."

"Even your niece, perhaps? Come on, Aunt Ella, tell me, am I a likely murderess?"

"Certainly not. I'd as soon suspect myself as you. No, the murderer was one of the men."

"How about Sophie? We mustn't forget her."

"That poor little blue-eyed darling? I should say not." Miss Singlefoot was indignant at the thought.

"Well, if she didn't, only her husband and Tom are left. Of course, either of them might have done it."

"Mona, you are generally very clear-headed but I feel that you are making a slip here. There is another person on this boat who has never been seriously questioned as far as I can see. Everyone else is held as a potential murderer, a thief, and yet the person who may have had as much cause walks along under the least suspicion."

"Who in the world are you talking about? I thought everyone had been questioned thoroughly."

"You don't know? Well, then I feel it my duty to tell you. The man is—"

Just at this moment a knock on the door interrupted them.

"Who is it?" called Miss Singlefoot, straightening her rumpled dress.

"It's Dr. Bradshaw. Could I have a little talk with you?"

Miss Singlefoot stared at her niece.

"Speaking of the devil—" she whispered shrilly before opening the door to admit her caller.

Mona couldn't help wondering how long he had been standing there before he knocked. She had no illusions now about anyone on the creaking little boat.

CHAPTER XXI
"I WON'T KEEP SILENT"

They told the doctor of the conversation between Jane Davet and Mr. Spencer.

"So that's why the maid was nervous," he ejaculated at the end of their story. "Jack Spencer is mixed up in this. However, I don't think he's the real murderer. He's probably merely an accomplice. It's evident that two are at this crooked business. Two murders and a theft are more than one man can handle."

"Perhaps," said Mona in an unconvinced tone. "But who do you think is the real murderer?" Dr. Bradshaw seemed so sure of himself now, while at first he had impressed her as being uncertain and helpless in the face of big issues. It was queer this change in him. Had he been playing a part in the beginning, or was he playing one now?

"Tom Amory has been telling me about something inexplicable that he encountered last night. He said that he left his room to investigate strange noises that he heard in the hall and in the course of his prowling knocked on Colonel Worthington's door. Colonel Worthington opened it immediately and claimed he was on the verge of doing some investigating himself when Mr. Amory knocked. So far, so good—but here is what doesn't sound plausible. Colonel Worthington told Amory that he had gone to bed but hadn't been able to sleep—that he had tossed about and, finally, had gotten up, turned on the light and started to read. The lights went off suddenly and not wanting to read by candle-light he decided to try sleeping again. It was then he heard some one moving about in the hall. Amory said Colonel Worthington wore pyjamas and this substantiated his story. But he also said that the man's hair was neatly combed, which condition would have been impossible had he been tossing about in bed."

"Of course, you know," commented Mona, "that Tom may have been inventing all this rigmarole."

"He may have," returned the doctor, "but I don't believe it. He sounded sincere enough to me. No, I feel sure he was telling the truth."

"Even if he were," insisted Mona, "there might be a plausible explanation for Colonel Worthington's hair being in place."

"That's not all I'm going by. Remember you found the empty jewel case in his room. Spencer probably stole the jewels and Colonel Worthington was hiding the case for him."

"But why keep the case? Why didn't the thief throw it overboard?"

"He was afraid of being seen."

"Rot," snapped Mona. "The jewel case was put there to cast suspicion on the Colonel."

"Then," continued Dr. Bradshaw, "the fact that Colonel Worthington needs money badly makes murder for theft the more plausible. But he reckoned without me." The fat little man was as pompous and assuming as he had been meek and intimidated two days earlier.

Mona wondered if the heat had gone to his head or if he honestly thought he'd found the guilty person? She didn't understand the doctor. He was like a balloon, inflated one minute, deflated the next.

"I have a feeling," she said, "that the answer to all this is very simple and lies in the person of John Stewart, Celia's cousin, and part heir to her estate. He's either on this boat in disguise or the evil spirit behind who's driving some poor harassed soul to murder. The jewel theft may simply be a blind to cover a deeper cause."

"There might be another meaning to the conversation I overheard between Mr. Spencer and the maid," put in Miss Singlefoot suddenly. "Mr. Spencer may have discovered the true identity of one of the passengers, Colonel Worthington perhaps, and may be blackmailing him as a consequence. Perhaps he needs money to pay his gambling debts and this is an easy way to get it."

"Easy way nothing," retorted Mona, shaking her head vigorously. "He's taking a bigger chance than if he put his head in a lion's mouth." She fondled the bruised spots on her neck. "Blackmail on his part would simply be a case of signing his own death warrant."

"Didn't Mr. Amory say that this Stewart fellow has been in India quite a lot?" asked Miss Singlefoot, pleating and re-pleating a small handkerchief with her long, bony fingers. Then she added quite as if it were of no importance at all. "Colonel Worthington lived in India too. He told us so."

Dr. Bradshaw stared fixedly at this often foolish, sometimes wise woman. He believed she held the key.

"I have been talking to Professor Cross about you," he remarked simply. If Miss Singlefoot had received an electric shock she couldn't have shown more surprise. She sat bolt upright in her chair. A look almost of terror came into her eyes and then disappeared as suddenly as it had come.

"I don't understand," she said, and then went on fiercely. "If it's the old Haines case, I didn't know what he was talking about this morning and I don't know now."

"That's not it," said the doctor. "I'm not interested in any allusions to that case. I don't know any more about it than you say you do."

"What is it then?" she asked.

"I want to know what you heard during the night before Miss Lawton's murder? Something took place in the corridor. What was it?"

Miss Singlefoot was nervous. She kept blinking her eyes rapidly like a baby with the sun in its face. She glanced at Mona but received no encouragement from that source.

"Can't you wait, Doctor," she pleaded, "until we get off this awful boat? Ask me tomorrow at Assuan. I'll tell you then."

"You may not be able to if we wait. I believe if definite action is not taken soon it will be too late. Too late for someone, maybe you."

"But if I tell you, I may be knifed in the back or bitten by some loathsome viper. I'm afraid." She rocked in her chair, her knees stiff against each other. "I'm afraid," she repeated, moaning unconsciously to herself.

"I promise you that nothing will happen to you if you tell me," urged the doctor, looking at Mona appealingly. "I'll see that you're protected if I have to station an Arab at your door."

"Oh, don't do that," gasped Miss Singlefoot. "I'd be mortally afraid of one of those brutes. Oh, what shall I do? Mona, you help me. Shall I tell him?"

Mona turned to Dr. Bradshaw.

"Do you think we'll reach Assuan tonight?" she asked in a steady voice.

He went to the window and looked out.

"If the storm passes, and it has already moderated considerably, I think perhaps we can make it. I'm going to do my best. We certainly don't want another night of this."

"I'd tell him, then, Aunt Ella. I think you're safe enough in the daytime if you stay with the crowd."

"All right," said the harassed woman. "Promise you won't tell the others?" She glanced at the pudgy little man sharply.

"I promise," he returned gravely.

"I had gone to sleep," she began, her eyes on the windowpane, "and was dreaming pleasantly when the sound of voices coming from the next cabin awakened me. Someone—a woman—was talking loudly and angrily but I couldn't pick out the words. The walls were too thick. Then I heard a door open so I decided to get up and see who the night visitor was. I put on my dressing gown and peered out my door. A flood of light coming from Celia's room illuminated the hall and I saw Colonel Worthington standing there in his bathrobe. I wasn't able to see Miss Lawton, who was apparently just inside the door, but I couldn't help overhearing what she said. She was angry and her words were low and distinct. I remember them exactly. 'My decision is final,' she said, 'I won't keep silent any longer!' Colonel Worthington stood looking at her, his face red with anger, and for a moment I thought he'd strike her—however, he controlled himself and then turned without a word and started down the hall. I closed my door for I didn't want to be seen, but I stood in the dark until the sound of Colonel Worthington's footsteps died away. And that's all I heard."

"So Miss Lawton was holding something over Colonel Worthington's head. Now, I wonder what it was?" muttered Dr. Bradshaw softly.

"The storm is over," remarked Mona suddenly, pointing to the window. "We can make Assuan now, can't we, Doctor?"

"It won't be my fault if we don't," he answered grimly, and with a nod to them both left the room.

"What was that bulge in his back pocket?" asked Miss Singlefoot, her eyes big as saucers.

"That," said Mona, curiously sober, "was a gun."

CHAPTER XXII
A WARNING

Mona stooped and picked up something green and square and shining. Cat's eyes shining at her out of the dark. She put it in her pocket, that little hard bit of color, and proceeded on to the dining-room. The storm was over and the Arabs had, at last, gotten together a belated luncheon.

"Everyone will sit at the center table," Dr. Bradshaw was saying as she entered the room. "I am using two of the waiters to pole because I want to make Assuan soon after dark. I hope you don't mind. We can be served quicker if we sit together."

"Lot of good it would do us if we did mind," muttered Jack Spencer under his breath.

Mona looked around the table. Professor Cross, taciturn and preoccupied, Aunt Ella, nervous and gaunt, Tom, haggard and brooding, Jack Spencer, frowning and no longer urbane, Sophie, limp and sullen, Jimmie, agitated and plainly hungry, Dr. Bradshaw, standing beside an empty chair, unutterably weary.

"We are all here but Colonel Worthington," he said. "I wonder where he is?"

"On deck, reading," offered Tom Amory, without glancing at the doctor. "He told Professor Cross he wasn't eating lunch. Said he had nervous indigestion."

"Yes, I lent him a book to take his mind off himself and the whole situation," remarked the Professor.

"As if anything could," muttered Sophie bitterly. She raised the glass of water to her lips, and then made a wry face. "I'd like some ice water," she said.

"I'm very sorry," returned Dr. Bradshaw, "but there is no ice water."

"What's become of it?" snapped Jack Spencer. "There was plenty last night."

"I have had to use the ice for preservation purposes," he answered pointedly. Everyone caught his meaning except Miss Singlefoot.

"I don't understand," she said.

"In other words, he has cut up the ice in chunks, put the chunks in buckets, placed the buckets in the two death chambers. Is that clear?" asked Professor Cross callously, "or shall I explain just why the ice was needed?"

"For God's sake, don't." Sophie's voice was shrill. "I'm a nervous wreck now from thinking of it."

"Here we are," said Tom, pushing his salad plate from him in disdain, "and one of us a murderer and thief. Pleasant thought, isn't it?"

"Not half as pleasant as the idea that one of us will be in jail tomorrow," returned Jack Spencer. "I'll sure be there to gloat over the damned cuss."

"Are you certain you won't be the damned cuss, as you call him?" Professor Cross's lips clucked over each word.

"Asking me or yourself?"

Professor Cross refused to answer. He seemed to be thinking about something else.

"Won't the hotel keeper at Assuan be surprised when he hears the details?" Tom laughed harshly. "He wished us a pleasant trip, too."

"I bet he'll be mad as hell," said Jack Spencer. "He'll have two less customers—Celia and the murderer won't require rooms."

"I wish I were packed," sighed Sophie. "I want to be the first to put my foot off this boat. No more trips to the Sudan for me."

"Does anyone know where John Stewart is living now?" asked Professor Cross suddenly, staring at the circle of strained faces.

"I saw him the day he left the States," Sophie's voice was strangely light. "I don't know where he was going. He wouldn't say."

"He's still in India for all I know," said Tom. "There's one fellow who'll be glad to hear the news. He and Celia never got along any too well anyway and this sudden inheritance of his will be a boon from heaven. He was always a wild lot, living with first one woman, then another. That's the reason he and Celia didn't hit it off. She hated men who didn't play fair with women."

"She certainly had a lot of nerve feeling that way. I never knew her to have any scruples when she played with men." Sophie met Tom's eyes unflinchingly. "Celia was a flirt," she said deliberately.

Tom half rose from his chair and then without a word sank back and continued eating. She was malicious, this Worthington woman, but he couldn't deny her statement. Celia, so dear and so far away from him forever, had been a flirt.

"Can we get off as soon as we reach Assuan, Doctor?" Miss Single-foot's hair was stringing about her face. She had not used a curling iron on it for two days and the heat had taken out all the wave.

"I'm afraid not. When the boat docks I'll send a runner to the hotel. You'll have to wait until the Company's officials and the English police representatives get aboard. From then on we'll do as they say. The whole affair will be out of my hands, thank God."

"I shall be glad to eat decent meals again," said Sophie, eyeing the rice pudding in disgust. "No wonder Charlie is sick. This food is enough to poison anyone."

"Perhaps Colonel Worthington is suffering from an over-worked conscience, not a bad stomach," remarked Jack Spencer, ironically.

"Just what do you mean by that?" Sophie glared at him. She was like a tiger defending her young. Her blue eyes sparkled dangerously.

"A lot, my dear lady. A lot, none of which I care to repeat."

Mona was watching Sophie. Did she suspect her husband of being the killer? Did she know something that the others didn't? Her room was adjoining his. What had she discovered?

"The murderer possesses a pair of leather gloves with which he handled the asp." Professor Cross paused to let his words sink in. "When we find the gloves the search is over."

"No doubt," retorted Jack Spencer with heavy sarcasm. "But we all have leather gloves tucked away somewhere in our baggage. I do for one and I'm sure the rest of you will say the same."

Mona broke into the conversation.

"Where is your emerald?" she asked casually, pointing to Sophie's right hand. Around the third finger was a white line but no ring. "You haven't lost it, have you?"

Sophie glanced down at her hand. Mona got the impression somehow that she winced at the question.

"Of course not," she replied. "I didn't think to put it on after I washed my hands for lunch. It's down in my cabin."

"Or so we trust," said Professor Cross, fingering his clean-shaven chin. "It may have gone the way of all jewels lately. Perhaps the thief visited you too. Life is so uncertain—on a floating morgue." His words were utterly devoid of emotion. He spoke as one would expect an automaton to speak.

"A nice fat emerald would pay a lot of bills," murmured Jack Spencer with what was apparently irrelevance. Sophie looked up at him sharply. He was so exasperating. How could she have ever liked him?

"I'm going out in the air," snapped Miss Singlefoot. "This smelly old room is a dungeon of heat. Come along Mona."

But Mona didn't move. She was thinking of an orderly man suddenly becoming disorderly, of piles of unpaid bills, of cat's eyes, green eyes peering at her out of the dark. They were flashing a warning, those eyes, a warning which she couldn't fathom. She was afraid—afraid and muddled, for she didn't understand why Sophie had lied about the emerald ring.

CHAPTER XXIII
GATEWAY OF THE DEAD

Mona's mind went back to a missing soap box. If she only knew who had stolen it from the little blue bag. She tried to remember whose room had been down the corridor from her aunt's in the Assuan hotel, but it was useless. She simply couldn't remember. Her mind kept going back to Colonel Worthington. He recalled memories of her childhood summers spent on Cape Cod. Where was the connection? Why should he, a Britisher, take her mind back to America? She smiled to herself. It was silly not to have thought of it before. The link lay in his soft English accents that were so Bostonian in quality.

Why was Sophie bitter and indifferent one minute, and the next almost consumingly on the defensive? If someone had stolen her emerald, why did she try to keep it secret? The answer seemed obvious. She knew the thief and murderer, and knowing him, she wanted to protect him. She was making a desperate effort to save Charlie Worthington, her husband, from the electric chair or whatever they did to one in Egypt.

Mona tried to visualize the direction from which the soap box had been thrown. It could easily have come from Colonel Worthington's cabin.

Someone was calling her name. She looked up from her thoughts to see an Arab standing beside her chair. "What is it?" she asked.

"Dr. Bradshaw wants you come to his office."

Mona glanced at her watch. It was ten minutes to three. She ground her cigarette in a little copper ashtray and walked briskly out of the smoking lounge. She felt it in her bones. Something was going to happen.

"I have decided," said Dr. Bradshaw, closing the door behind Mona, and rubbing his hands together nervously, "not to delay matters any longer. I am going to call Colonel Worthington in here and confront him with the evidence we have against him. What do you think?"

"I don't know," answered Mona slowly. "We wouldn't want to make a mistake."

"That's why something should be done now before another mistake is made. I'm frankly afraid to wait."

"Is it safe?" argued Mona. "Why not watch Colonel Worthington carefully until we dock and when outside protection comes, accuse him."

"No," returned the doctor, shortly, "this is the time. I wonder where he is?"

"In a chair, reading, on the deck just above this room. I saw him as I came by. I'll call him for you."

Dr. Bradshaw started to remonstrate but Mona was gone. She felt fairly secure as long as it was daylight.

She ran lightly up the steps despite the early afternoon's heat. Nervous excitement was numbing her senses to the ever-growing fatigue.

She could see him sitting in a deck chair, fifteen feet from where she stood. He was in the same position as when she had passed him five minutes earlier. How could he read in such heat?

"Colonel Worthington," she called softly. No need to walk down that sun-baked deck. Besides, it was safer this way.

He did not answer. His head was bent over the book which he held with both hands.

"Colonel Worthington!" she repeated, louder this time. Still there was no answer. Exasperating man. It was silly to pretend he couldn't hear. She started toward him and then stopped suddenly in her tracks. Little chills of fear raced up and down her spine. She stood poised like some wild animal who has suddenly caught a scent spelling danger.

She could see the open pages of his book. Bright sunlight flooded them. No sensible person would submit his eyes to the task of reading in the burning African sun.

Something was wrong. Awareness of it paralyzed her for the moment. Queer, how intent he was. There was a strange rigidity to his position. He sat like a man who would never be disturbed again.

Mona wanted to scream but she couldn't. Her tongue was a frozen lump against the hot roof of her mouth. Instead of running down the stairs as her wildly thumping heart dictated, she walked slowly toward the silent figure.

"Colonel Worthington!" she called in a voice closely resembling a strangle. "Oh, Colonel Worthington!"

Only the never-ending hum of the paddle-wheel answered her. She couldn't see his face. It was hidden from her eyes. She looked down at his chest. There was no movement.

She screamed his name. Still no answer. She grasped his shoulders in her strong fingers and shook them. With the rigidity of a marble statue the body slid down in the chair. It lay quiet and flat against unyielding wooden slats.

Colonel Worthington was dead. No one could accuse him now of murder or theft.

Mona felt someone staring at her. Alive, curious eyes. She looked up. Professor Cross was standing in the doorway, motionless. He was like a menacing figure in a nightmare.

"You can't wake him?" he asked, his voice penetrating the silence sharply.

"No," she said dully, "I can't. He's dead."

Professor Cross came noiselessly to her side. He touched the dead man's cheek.

"Quite dead," he agreed. "Only the dead could be cool on this hot deck."

Professor Cross' eyes leered at Mona like horrible flames of heat striking her face.

"He was dead when you reached him." It was not a question or a statement, merely a collection of words. "Of course."

Professor Cross' white fingers were moving rapidly over Colonel Worthington's inert frame. Those fingers fascinated Mona. She thought of tarantulas eager with their poison. There was a difference though. Tarantulas' claws are dark and hairy, not gray and bloodless.

One inhuman hand came to rest on the open book. There was a motion as if to pull it from the dead fingers.

"I wouldn't disturb anything," warned Mona.

"It's my book," returned Professor Cross with no emotion in his flat voice.

Mona laughed suddenly. A queer little laugh. It was all too ridiculous. Coincidences like this shouldn't happen.

"Look—the name of the book," she pointed to four words in big letters at the head of the page, *Gateway of the Dead*. She laughed again. It was a horrible jest.

"Quite appropriate, I should say," remarked Professor Cross. "But ghastly, too—quite ghastly."

"We must tell Dr. Bradshaw." Mona had the sickening sensation that she was going to faint. She turned away, her face pallid.

"Is it necessary?" murmured that thin, thoughtful man, mechanically, as one in a nightmare.

Mona looked down at her watch. The hands pointed to mid-afternoon.

"It is three o'clock," she said, "and three are dead."

CHAPTER XXIV
"THAT DEVIL GOT HIM"

Dr. Bradshaw told Sophie that her husband was dead.

"Charlie—dead?" There was unbelief in her tone.

"Yes, Madam, we discovered him dead in a deck chair."

Sophie was standing now, staring at the doctor. Her face was white, her hands clenched.

"Take me to him," she commanded.

Dr. Bradshaw started to object.

"Take me to him," she repeated, her voice like lead.

The body had been carried down to the empty stateroom on the lower deck next to Miss Singlefoot's.

The other passengers, talking excitedly, were congregated in the corridor outside of the death chamber. They became silent as the two approached. Sophie did not seem to notice them. Her head was bent and she walked stiffly in the manner of one hypnotized.

Dr. Bradshaw unlocked the door and she followed him into the room. Unerringly her gaze went to the sheeted form on the bed. She moved swiftly to its side and pulled down the covering. She was silent for a moment, then, turning her head, asked through blue lips, "Did he die a natural death?"

"He was murdered, Madam," came the answer.

Sophie recoiled as if from a blow in the face. "How?"

"He was stabbed in the back of the neck, in the same manner as Abdu. He died instantly."

Sobs were wracking Sophie's tense body. She leaned over and kissed the dead lips, bluer than her own.

Suddenly a fierce anger seemed to seize her. Her eyes sparkled dangerously while great blobs of tears streamed through powder-caked channels down her face. She had lost her pose of inertia and was now talking brokenly to herself.

"That devil got him—he got him." Her voice ended in a whisper. Apparently she had forgotten Dr. Bradshaw. Her head was thrown back, her hands clasping and unclasping convulsively. Without warning she swayed weakly against the bed and the doctor sprang to her side.

"You must go to your cabin," he said gently, "and rest. I'll give you something to make you sleep."

Sophie's blue eyes were suddenly those of an obedient child's. They were almost eager.

"Yes, I want to sleep," she said, "I want to sleep forever. Maybe I can forget then."

"What do you mean by 'that devil got him?' Do you know who killed your husband?" asked the doctor softly. He supported the hysterical woman with his strangely long arms.

Her eyes were blank.

"I don't know," she answered dully. "All I know is I'm tired. Dreadfully tired."

They got her to her room and Miss Singlefoot and Mona helped her into bed. Soon Dr. Bradshaw returned with the sleeping draught. He watched her drink it.

"You'll feel better for this," he said soothingly. "Just go to sleep. Miss Singlefoot will sit here with you."

Sophie opened her eyes and peered up at the doctor.

"Thank you," she murmured wearily. Her eyes were searching for Miss Singlefoot, who stood behind the fat little man.

"It will be nice of you to sit with me." Her words trailed off into a whisper. She was falling asleep.

Dr. Bradshaw and Mona tiptoed out of the room. Miss Singlefoot locked the door after them and settled herself in the one lone rocker. The cabin was hot and uncomfortable. But, as far as that was concerned, so was her own. The atmosphere from the neighboring death chambers seemed to have settled like a pall on her stuffy little bedroom. It was thoughtless of the doctor to have put Colonel

Worthington's body in the empty room next to hers. He might have had some consideration for her nervous system. Hadn't she gone through the shock of discovering the second dead body? Any one would have been upset at opening a door expecting to find tea dishes and instead meeting a dead Arab face to face. She could see those eyes now, staring at her in the dim light. They had shone in his Semitic face like phosphorus on a dark night. She shivered at the memory and looked back to see that the door was closed behind her. One thought consoled her. On this side of the boat, at least, there were no dead. Sophie's face was pale but she was alive. Miss Single-foot knew that for she could see the sheet moving above her tired body.

"Poor dear," she muttered softly, "she'll be so alone now that her husband is dead."

CHAPTER XXV
A PUZZLE OF EIGHT

Of one thing Mona still felt certain. John Stewart had something to do with it all. He was either on the boat in disguise or it was his malicious influence that was dealing out the death potion so generously. This conviction came to Mona not suddenly nor from a collection of cold facts, but rather from an ever-increasing assemblage of vague impressions and here and there a startling intuitive flash.

Now what did she know about this John Stewart? Mona scribbled a few notes as she thought. Perhaps from white paper and black ink might come the answer.

Sophie had contributed to the scant information concerning him. She said that women constituted a great part of John Stewart's life and although entirely unscrupulous, he had a way with them. Strange that he and Celia hadn't hit it off together, for according to Sophie, they were two of a kind.

Tom had said he was a newspaper man originally from Boston, that he was somewhere around forty-five years of age, and that he had been in India for the past few years. Celia had not liked him. Perhaps he knew this and as a natural consequence did not waste any love on her. If Celia left no will, at her death half of her fortune would go to her cousin. Was it hard to believe that he murdered her for her money?

But if he were the murderer he must be on the boat masquerading under another name, and if so, what was it? Only five white men were left and one of them was not a passenger. Perhaps that was why Charlie Worthington had died. Perhaps the Colonel knew the identity of John Stewart and was threatening to make it known. What did

Celia mean the night she told Colonel Worthington that she would remain silent no longer? Did Celia recognize her cousin? Could Colonel Worthington, by any chance, have been John Stewart? Mona thought so before his death, but now she had changed her mind.

It was a shame that she didn't know more about Celia's life. It seemed that Sophie and Celia spent their early childhood together in a small town in New York State. Celia had said once that her father's life had been spent as a banker, taking care of people's money, while Sophie's father had been a doctor, taking care of people's physical infirmities. Mona's impression was that Celia had always had the best of everything— of clothes, education, travel and friends. Could it be that someone not quite so well off was envious of her good fortune, and murdered her from sheer jealousy? Sophie, for instance. Sophie, who from infancy had played second fiddle. Mona shrugged her shoulders. She was unable to conceive of wholesale murder for the sake of a covetousness which in the end wouldn't be satisfied. No, she clung to the theory that the murder was precipitated from uncontrollable greed for Celia's riches. And this theory definitely involved John Stewart.

Mona felt that the murders of Celia and Colonel Worthington were closely connected. Just how, she didn't know. If the latter had been a rich man, suspicion would naturally have fallen on his wife, but he was decidedly not wealthy. He was deeply in debt and unless he carried a big life insurance Sophie would not profit by his death.

What connection had Jack Spencer with it all? And what part did the maid, Jane Davet, play? And were the jewels stolen to cover up the real motive for the murder and to divert attention from the actual murderer, or were they stolen separately and before the first murder took place? Mona discountenanced the theory that Celia was killed for her jewels. They were probably worth a great deal of money but in comparison with an estate of millions of dollars they were but a drop in the bucket.

Five white men on the boat. If the guilty one were a man, who was it?

Not Jimmie Bean. It was ridiculous to consider him. Mona simply couldn't share her aunt's suspicions concerning that care-free boy.

Somehow now she didn't think that Tom, Celia's fiancé and long-enduring lover, was the one either. His devotion had been too loyal and too unselfish. He was the junior member of a great engineering firm whose business was chiefly concerned with building dams in far-off corners of the earth. On account of the flooding of the rivers at different seasons of the year, work often had to be discontinued for several months at a time. It was during these months that he accompanied Celia on her practically perpetual tour of the ultra-fashionable pleasure resorts. Sometimes her whims carried her to America but more often to the shores of the Mediterranean. Of course, he had written her a disagreeable letter on the night before the series of murders began. And that letter had disappeared. One couldn't be sure just how.

Mona remembered the thin blue envelopes she had taken from Jack Spencer's writing case. She searched for them in her desk drawers. Ah, there they were. She should have thought of them before.

She pursed her lips as she examined the contents of the three envelopes. Duns, all of them, sent out from a gambling house in St. Jean de Luz. Jack had said this was his first winter in Egypt for a long time, that he had come principally for his health. Mona smiled cynically to herself. It was easy to imagine that the Continent got a little hot for him and that his breath came easier in Egypt. The bills called for pretty big sums. If he didn't have the money to pay them, he was in a desperate situation. Maybe that was what he meant when he said to Jane, "I had to do it." Perhaps, but did he mean that he had stolen the jewels, killed Celia and eventually the two others, or did he mean something entirely different and unconnected with the depressing affairs at hand?

Professor Cross puzzled her, too. He was always turning up at the most unexpected times. She knew very little about his life other than he was a great traveler, writer, and archaeologist. He had been in all parts of the world many times. He might well have been the nocturnal visitor to Nusa, the snake charmer. But it was not clear how he would profit by either Celia's or Charlie Worthington's death.

Abdu, of course, was in the picture merely by accident. There was little doubt that he was blackmailing the murderer. The torn bank note in his dead fingers told that story. He was standing, probably by appointment, at the head of the stairs and when he opened his hand behind him to take the hush money, was stabbed in a vital spot at the base of the brain.

The only other man was Dr. Bradshaw. He claimed that he had been a government doctor in England, a surgeon on several large transatlantic liners, and a quarantine officer at some port in Australia. He said that he was in Africa now for his health, and had welcomed the job of captain of this hideous little boat. Mona had the impression that ten years previous, before his health broke, he was an attractive man. Queer, the way some people gained weight after tuberculosis set in. Aunt Ella seemed to think that he had a big finger in the pie but Mona couldn't quite place him in the scheme of things. She did remember hearing several years ago about some ship doctor who was discovered to be a professional thief. It was possible that Dr. Bradshaw was a thief and murderer as well. Certainly his salary wasn't large enough to satisfy him if he had luxurious tastes. Aunt Ella was sometimes clever in her rather blundering, foolish way. Perhaps she was right. It was evident that a professional criminal was aboard for, if Tom had told the truth about the past night, someone on the boat possessed and was using a burglar's device for opening locked doors.

Mona's mind reverted to the emerald ring and to Sophie, who pretended she didn't know it was lost. What did that mean? It was a puzzle and Mona felt strangely helpless and far from the answer to it all.

CHAPTER XXVI
IN THE ICE PANTRY

Dr. Bradshaw gave Mona the impression that he was perturbed. He would have given anyone that impression. His naturally florid face was two shades more brilliant than usual, his formerly immaculate linen suit had lost completely its freshness and on the whole he was like a fat bunch of carrots in an agricultural exhibit—wilted at the end of the day.

He kept striding up and down the floor of the narrow confines of the ship's office. His trousers were baggy at the knees and on each was a suggestion of dust as if he had been kneeling somewhere. Finally, he stopped in his determined promenade to stand before Mona, a fierce light in his protruding eyes.

"I tell you, I'm a ruined man. I had fears of it at first but now I'm certain. One of His Majesty's subjects, dead—murdered—on my boat and I didn't do a thing to prevent it. Not a thing."

"What could you have done?" asked Mona softly.

He stared at her. His lips were strangely moist and purple. Mona didn't like corpulent men.

"I don't suppose I could have done anything," he said, still staring at her.

Animals are so much better off than human beings. They suffer only momentarily from a present evil. They never look into a future which presents to them certain misfortune and unhappiness. The doctor seemed to be looking now upon a scene that was as hopeless as it was inevitable. His eyes were cloudy with misgivings.

"Dead," he continued, "dead right under our eyes. I wouldn't doubt that everyone on this boat passed his chair between the time of the murder and three o'clock. Perhaps they spoke to him. To a casual passer-by he looked perfectly natural, slumped in the chair, a book in his hands. By the way," he stopped speaking for a moment, his face reflecting aroused interest, "it was strangely fitting, the book he was reading—*Gateway of the Dead*. Do you suppose the criminal had the peculiar sense of humor which would prompt him to give his victim such a book and then murder him while he read it?"

"It was Professor Cross who lent him the book," Mona reminded the doctor. "And Professor Cross has just such a sense of humor."

Dr. Bradshaw was shaking his head.

"Now that I've come to think about it," he said, "that book is not such an unusual one, even for a dead man to be reading. All this country is described by authors as being the entrance to the realm of the dead. The notion comes from the thousands of tombs along the banks of the Nile."

"You're right," agreed Mona. "There's probably no relation. It's a fantastic theory arising from three fantastic and elusive murders. By the way, I wonder what weapon was used to stab Abdu and Colonel Worthington?"

"I meant to tell you, Miss Case. I have discovered that both the ice picks which are usually kept in the pantry are missing. There is little doubt in my mind that these were the weapons used. They were both small, slender picks which, if wielded with any force at all in the vicinity of the *medulla oblongata*, would pierce the spinal column, causing instant death. In Abdu's case the amount of blood was small and in all probability the blow was not as clean as it might have been. I think it due to the fact that the murderer stood on a lower level than Abdu, who was evidently standing in the doorway facing the rail of the boat. It must have been a trifle awkward to strike with deadly force at such an angle. Colonel Worthington's position was a more auspicious one; that is, more auspicious for the murderer, who, slipping up behind him, struck him while he was reading. The unfortunate man's neck was laid quite bare since his head was bent over the book."

"The ice picks were thrown overboard in both instances?"

"Undoubtedly, Miss Case."

"And there are no more ice picks?"

"No more."

Mona was smiling a crooked little smile.

"Then we'll have no more murders," she said.

Dr. Bradshaw shook his head wearily.

"Nothing to that idea. With so fertile a brain as the murderer has, other weapons could be found. The first was, you remember, an asp—a very efficient and quiet instrument of death."

"Doesn't it appear to you that the first death was premeditated, while the next two were emergency affairs? The first murder must have been elaborately planned and executed, while the next two were done on the spur of the moment. Abdu was a danger which cropped up unforeseen and unprovided for in the shape of black-mail and had to be dealt with quickly. God only knows why Colonel Worthington was killed. But I don't believe his death was necessarily planned when Celia's was."

Mona stopped suddenly, a devastating thought taking possession of her.

"I told you," she said slowly, her lips dry from excitement, "about overhearing the snake charmer's conversation with his mysterious visitor. You remember, he gave that visitor not one viper, but two. If the unknown visitor is the murderer, another viper is hidden somewhere on this boat and another person marked for death."

Dr. Bradshaw mopped his dripping forehead.

"I hope to God you're wrong," he said. "I've already lost my job, and if this slaughter keeps up I'll lose my mind. I really can't stand any more of it."

Mona looked at him as, fretting and fuming, he strode about the room on short, fat legs. She might have pitied him if she were sure he was not cloaking the real cause of his worry. Was he the criminal fearing conviction or did he fear a nearer and surer fate? Was he, by any chance, the one marked for the second viper? Questions crowded her mind that she might have asked the harassed man but she didn't.

"Where is the ship's ice box situated?" she queried instead.

Mild surprise was in his voice as he answered her. "In a small pantry directly back of the dining room.

"Does the little window you come to just before you reach the dining-room door open into it?"

"Why, yes, it does. You pass by it on your way to meals."

"I wonder," said Mona, her eyes shining luminously, "if you could tell me just where in that pantry the ice picks were kept?" Emotion rode rampant through her words.

Dr. Bradshaw hesitated for a moment before he answered.

"They hung, when not in use, on the wall just to the left of the ice box."

"And where is the ice box?" persisted Mona.

"Between the pantry door and the window. You could touch it from the deck outside."

"I see," said Mona. "Thank you." Her fingers closed over something small and hard in her linen pocket. Light, as Jimmie would say, was beginning to dawn and what it reflected was ugly and terrifying. She shuddered involuntarily and wished with all her heart that she were back at home in her safe little newspaper office.

CHAPTER XXVII
MISS SINGLEFOOT SCREAMS AGAIN

Miss Singlefoot dozed in her chair. Her flat chest was rising and falling rhythmically while her head, usually held high above a thin, scrawny neck, was gradually dropping lower and lower. Suddenly all the muscles in the upper part of her body relaxed and allowed her V-shaped chin to drop sharply forward. With a little cry of pain she half rose from her chair, one hand involuntarily going to her chin, the other to a cluster of diamonds she wore on the front of her dress. Some of the stones must have been loose, for the pin had pricked her chin. It had made a deep scratch on the flesh which she could feel with her long, bony fingers. Drat it all, she had been sleeping so peacefully, too.

Sophie had not stirred. Miss Singlefoot peered at the woman's face. It was chalky white with not a touch of color to relieve the paleness. She wondered why Sophie hadn't used any rouge or lipstick. It was more fitting, of course, that she hadn't, her husband being dead and all that, but still, she would have looked more lifelike with some on.

Wonder what it was the doctor had given her to make her sleep. It couldn't have been morphine, for they always used a hypodermic needle for that. Now that nice doctor at home had given her something very strong once when she was suffering from a broken hip. Maybe Dr. Bradshaw had given Sophie the same thing. If she remembered rightly he called it peraldehyde or some such funny name. She wished she had been a man, she would have been a doctor. She liked to know these medical things. It was tremendously interesting. And one could do a lot of good with it. Take Sophie, for instance.

The poor thing had been so upset over her husband's death. She had seemed simply overcome. And now she was resting quietly, all from a little drink of medicine that the doctor had given her. Yes, it was wonderful. Irrelevantly, Miss Singlefoot wondered why the government didn't use medicine more often to punish criminals. Why not poison a murderer instead of hanging him? It certainly would be less trouble.

The room was still and hot. She could almost see the waves of heat that pounded unmercifully against her tired head. She wouldn't mind being put to sleep like Sophie. But then, of course, doctors never give drugs unless the patient is hysterical or in pain.

She wondered what would be the first thing Sophie thought of when the effect of the medicine, whatever it was, wore off. Would it be of her husband? Would she see his cold lips with that drawn expression about them? Or would she think of something quite unimportant, perhaps something in her childhood?

They say you do think of the silliest things after taking a narcotic. Now she remembered that after her last operation she thought she was a minister standing in the pulpit preaching a sermon. The nurse kept asking her if she was all right, and she had said, "Yes, I'm all right with the Lord—all right with the Lord." Everyone had laughed at her. It may have seemed funny but they shouldn't have laughed. No one should laugh at religion, ever. So many people did—that's why awful things happened to them.

It was strange that Sophie didn't stir at all. She looked almost as dead as her husband. Of course, though, you could see her chest moving, if you watched closely. Miss Singlefoot was glad of that. It was no fun sitting beside someone who looked like a corpse, even if you knew she wasn't one.

So Sophie had been an actress in New York. She had been sorry to learn that, for she didn't think much of actresses in general. There must be a few nice ones, though. They couldn't all be bad. She didn't believe a woman with a questionable reputation could attract an Englishman enough for him to propose marriage. So much was demanded of their wives, yet the men themselves were frequently indiscreet.

Sophie had such pretty blue eyes. You could tell that she was a sweet, innocent person. Men always liked blondes, too. Miss

Singlefoot sighed. Perhaps if she had been a little blonder some man would have fallen for her like Colonel Worthington had for Sophie. Oh well, it was no use crying over spilt milk. Plenty of women, anyway, married after they were forty. That ugly Miss Hawkins at home got a man when she was fifty, if a day. She might find one yet. You never could tell in this life. Professor Cross seemed to like her. It was queer, though, his asking her about the Haines case. That had surprised her. These quiet people often come out with the most peculiar remarks.

She was getting fidgety. There was no telling when Sophie would wake up. She might as well be in her own cabin getting a little rest. Then she remembered suddenly that Colonel Worthington was laid out in the empty cabin next to hers. No, she couldn't sleep between two dead people. It was irritating, Dr. Bradshaw's putting the body in that room. One thing was sure, if the boat didn't get to Assuan that night, she'd ask to sleep somewhere else. Why not in Colonel Worthington's old cabin? She could be close to Sophie, too. Someone ought to sleep near her as long as she was so upset.

She'd ask the doctor as soon as she saw him. Colonel Worthington's cabin was such a nice big one, too. Probably much cooler than her own. She smiled grimly to herself. Less hot would have been better than cooler. No place on that boat was anywhere near cool, not even the ice chest. She wondered vaguely if the ice the doctor had put in Celia's cabin had all melted. No doubt it had.

Without realizing it she was nodding again. The atmosphere in the room was heavy. It was conducive to sleep. She was drifting off when suddenly, bang—went something in the next room, in Colonel Worthington's cabin.

She sat bolt upright in her chair, a stifled scream escaping her lips. How could anyone have gotten into the cabin? The door had been locked. She had heard the doctor say so. He had remarked that it was the only cabin with a Yale lock.

Miss Singlefoot wanted to peep in to see who had made the noise, but her limbs refused to work. She was frightened. What if it were the murderer? What was he doing in Colonel Worthington's room?

A horrible thought occurred to her. Suppose he were on his way into Sophie's room to kill the dead man's wife.

She stood up, her knees shaking like aspen trees in the wind. She must do something, anything, just so she kept the murderer out of that room.

She screamed out the words, her voice shrill and pipelike, "Who's in there?"

No answer. She stared helplessly at the closed door between the two rooms. If only a key were in the lock. She could turn it and then scream for help.

A click of metal striking against metal startled her taut nerves.

"Who's there?" she called again.

She could hear cautious steps. Her brain was too befuddled to place them. They might have been in the hall or the next room. It was too much for her—how could even a murderer get through a door fastened with a Yale lock? It was not possible.

Her pale blue eyes nearly popped from her head. A thought burned her with malignant flames. Only disembodied spirits go through locked doors. She forgot everything except the desire for escape. With trembling fingers she unlocked the hall door and, leaving it open behind her, ran into the corridor and up the stairs.

She screamed again and again as loudly as her fright-paralyzed vocal cords would permit. The whole boat was gathered at her side before she stopped.

CHAPTER XXVIII
THROUGH EVERY BARRIER

"Someone was in Colonel Worthington's cabin just a minute ago. I heard him." Miss Singlefoot looked around at the group of strained faces. Which of those mouths had refused to answer her? Which of these people was pretending a solicitude he didn't really feel?

"But it's impossible," said the doctor, a bit gruffly. "I locked that door myself on the inside less than an hour ago. No one could have gotten into the cabin unless he went through Mrs. Worthington's room first. That's out, for you, yourself, were there."

"Can't help it," snapped Miss Singlefoot. "I'm telling you I heard someone or something in that room. I was sitting beside Sophie, thinking how quiet everything was when suddenly something hit the floor in the next room. I called out and asked 'who's there' but got no answer. Then I heard some sort of metallic noise, not very loud, and some steps. I'm not sure where the steps were. About that time I rushed out of the room and up here." Miss Singlefoot stopped and looked at the doctor. Bewilderment and lack of understanding were stamped on her flushed face.

"I remembered," she said, "that the door had a Yale lock on it and that you had slipped the catch on the inside. That was what frightened me so. I didn't think anything human could get through the door."

Everyone caught the meaning of her words but no one would have admitted that they possessed the least foundation of truth. To have done so would have been mental suicide.

"Bosh," said Dr. Bradshaw emphatically. "If you heard a noise it was one of this crowd." He turned to the others. "Will you all, with the exception of Miss Case and Miss Singlefoot, go to the card room and wait for me? I have some questions I must ask you. I have put them off long enough. Meanwhile," he took Miss Singlefoot quietly by the arm, "I hope you won't mind going with me. I want to see if anything has been taken from Colonel Worthington's room. I don't want to leave it unlocked, either, with Mrs. Worthington down there alone." As an afterthought he added underneath his breath, "I suppose it is unlocked. Certainly it was a human being who made the noise, if any."

But the door was not unlocked. Dr. Bradshaw turned the knob between his strong fingers with no success.

"Queer," he muttered, "if you are sure you heard a noise."

"I heard a noise," insisted Miss Singlefoot.

They entered through Mrs. Worthington's room. She was, to all appearances, sleeping quietly, her face pale as the white coverlet. Mona closed the door softly between the two cabins.

"Sophie might as well get all the rest she can," she explained. "There may be more trouble on this boat, not to speak of what is in store for us when we reach civilization."

"I'm afraid you're right," said the doctor simply.

A frown settled on his face as he looked around the room.

"Nothing seems to be disturbed in here. You say it sounded like a book hitting the floor?"

"Yes, I think so. Of course, I can't be sure."

Two rather large books were on the bed-side table.

"It might have been one of these," suggested Mona, picking up a beautifully bound volume, and running her fingers through its leaves. "Some time or other this one has fallen. See the pages? They're crumpled and look as if someone had tried to straighten them out hurriedly."

"You're right," agreed the doctor. "It might easily have been knocked off. This table is crowded, what with the big chess box, a kodak and these books."

"The noise I heard was fairly loud," said Miss Singlefoot, "such as you'd expect from a book as heavy as that."

"But what do you suppose he was after?" asked Mona. "There's nothing of value in this cabin. Unless, of course, he didn't mean to stop here. He might have been after something in the next room. Do you suppose Sophie's life is in danger?"

"But why come through here?" argued the doctor. "Why not go to her room directly?"

"We'd better lock Sophie's outside door," said Miss Singlefoot, nervously. "For all we know that devil may be murdering her in her bed while we're jabbering in here." She was silently thanking her lucky stars that the book had hit the floor. Otherwise, she might have met the murderer. There was no doubt in her mind as to what would have been the result. She would have fainted from fright, if not actually died from the shock.

"That's a good idea," returned Mona, and slipped into Sophie's cabin.

"Why should anyone try to get through a door fastened with a Yale lock when the room that he really wants to enter has merely an ordinary lock on the door?" The doctor shook his head as if the problem were too much for him. "I don't understand how he opened this door anyway." He turned the knob and the door swung back on its hinges noiselessly. "Easy enough to get out once you're on the inside," he muttered.

"I wonder if those flakes of white paint mean anything?" Miss Singlefoot pointed to a heap of something on the threshold. It looked like sawdust and here and there a flake of white paint.

The doctor stepped out into the hall, his face a blank, covering whatever emotions he might have felt. He ran his fingers lightly along the white moulding where it was nailed against the sash of the door.

"Humph," he said, "this is where the powdered wood and paint came from. Some instrument has been pushed between here." He chewed his lip savagely. "I think I see how the door was opened." He turned the knob several times and pointed to the triangular-shaped piece of metal that projected from the lock. "Someone," he continued, "pushed a thin blade through against the end of this. A pallet knife would have done the trick easily."

Miss Singlefoot was fascinated.

"But who has such a thing as a pallet knife with him?"

"I wouldn't doubt there's an entire set of burglar's tools hidden around here somewhere," answered the doctor solemnly.

Mona, who had re-entered the room, agreed with him.

"Yes," she said, her voice unusually hard, "a locked door is no barrier on this boat."

CHAPTER XXIX
FRAYED NERVES

It was a bedraggled little group that huddled like sheep in the air-choked card room. No one had much to say. Each tried to give the impression of bored irritation and each, with one exception, failed. In any murder investigation even the innocent want a plausible explanation for their whereabouts at the crucial moment. And sometimes, even for the innocent, plausibility has to be faked. Only Professor Cross looked immaculate and unperturbed. He was either the credulous man who had absolutely nothing on his conscience or the cynic who, with perhaps a great deal to conceal, had foreseen and prepared for just such a meeting.

"This is devilish business," said Dr. Bradshaw, perspiration streaming down his plump, apple-like cheeks. "I don't mind telling you that I am through being polite. Three murders have been committed and from the looks of things there may be another. If any one of you feels that I am usurping my authority you are at liberty to report it to the ship's offices at Cairo. That won't bother me in the least. I will lose my job anyway. But between now and the time we dock at Assuan I am in full command of this show. I am the only one with a gun and if I see a single queer move on anyone's part I'm going to use it." He took a sinister-looking forty-five from his pocket and deposited it on the table before him.

No one spoke. Everyone seemed fascinated by the sight of the gun and Dr. Bradshaw's nervous fingers hovering so close to it.

"Miss Singlefoot was right," the doctor continued. "Someone was in the cabin adjoining Mrs. Worthington's. Someone who had no business being there."

"But how could he get in?" asked Tom dubiously. "I thought the door had a Yale lock on it."

"It did but the lock happened to be one of the less expensive ones with a triangular shaped bolt. The door sash, itself, is rather flimsy and for a clever crook with continental ideas it was simple." A grim humor pervaded his words. "The whole affair has been uncomplicated for him up to now. I've been running around aimlessly, allowing atrocities to happen. But if anything else occurs it will have to be done before us all. We're going to stay together or know the reason why. I have left a trustworthy Arab standing guard in the corridor on the lower deck before Mrs. Worthington's room. There is another Arab outside this door who can be counted on in case of an emergency. Incidentally," he turned to Mona, who was listening intently, "Miss Case, here, is assisting me in the investigation. She can go and come as she pleases."

Jack Spencer was looking at Mona, a peculiar expression on his face.

"I say now," he seemed to be embarrassed, "aren't you being a little prejudiced? Miss Case is charming and all that but why isn't she under suspicion like the rest of us? It's been rumored about that Celia was murdered for her money and that John Stewart, her cousin, is involved on the grounds that he will profit through his inheritance of half her estate. Let me remind you, in case you have forgotten, there is another heir—a young girl in the early twenties. I would say that you are insulting Miss Case's intelligence not to include her in the list of suspects, especially since she would fit in so nicely."

"That will be enough from you," stormed the doctor, his face the color of a hot young beet. "You'll have enough explaining to do on your own part without implicating anyone else. I repeat, Miss Case is assisting me and she is free to go about the ship as she chooses. I didn't say she was not a suspect. She is and so am I. I am not forgetting that for a minute."

"But really," said Professor Cross, his lips turning at the corners in a pinched smile, "you can't expect us to stay bunched in this inadequately sized room until we reach Assuan."

"This is where you'll stay—here or in the dining salon. We are going to have no more murders and no more thefts. Argument will be of no avail."

"My goodness gracious," gasped Miss Singlefoot. "How long before we get to Assuan?"

"If nothing happens, we'll be there by nine o'clock. It's five now."

"But Mona says she thinks the murderer has another snake with him and there's no telling what might happen if we stay together for four hours. He might get mad and let the snake loose and kill us all." Miss Singlefoot's voice ended in a wail. "A poisonous viper is worse than a gun any day."

Dr. Bradshaw for the moment was at a loss for words. Ludicrous and ridiculous as it sounded, there was cause for fear in what she said. An asp was small, dangerous and easily carried in a coat pocket. But no one wore gloves and only the most intrepid snake-charmer would dare touch an asp without them.

"I don't think you need worry," he said, his voice losing a little of its harshness, "for the present, at least."

Jack Spencer muttered something under his breath that sounded remarkably like "Silly ass." He was not in the habit of being browbeaten, as he termed it, or in the least restrained.

"What I want to know," Dr. Bradshaw's determined voice both ignored and dominated the murmur, "is where each of you were and what you were doing between one o'clock today and the time Miss Singlefoot screamed, which was, as nearly as I can remember, four-thirty."

"Why pick on that particular time?" asked Professor Cross, his face wearing a slightly bored, a quietly amused expression. "Why not go back further? You'll probably get as far and it will take up more of the unpleasant hours ahead."

"I thought," returned the doctor gently, "that you wanted to help me. You offered to once."

"I gave you some suggestions, yes. If you had followed them, perhaps this meeting would not be necessary. As it is, I think we're futilely involved in asking and answering questions, none of which you as the pseudo detective can check."

"Professor Cross," said the doctor in as dignified a tone as his rumpled appearance would permit, "I am disappointed in you. As a scholar and one with an analytical mind I expected an intelligent response rather than persistent opposition. Don't you want this affair cleared up without any more unfortunate occurrences?"

"Emphatically so. But how will our answering your questions help to do it? What the innocent person has to say concerning his whereabouts is of no consequence and the guilty man will not tell the truth."

"Nevertheless, I insist upon an inquiry," returned the doctor stubbornly. "We will begin by establishing, as clearly as possible, the location of each one from one o'clock to four-thirty. I say one o'clock for Colonel Worthington had been dead close onto two hours when his body was discovered. And just to make it fair all the way around I will account for myself first of all. I was in Miss Single-foot's cabin, having a chat with her and Miss Case, until one-thirty. From there I went straight to the dining-room, by way of the shore stairs, thereby not passing Colonel Worthington's chair at all. I was in the dining-room and kitchen until about a quarter to three when I went to my office, which is, as you know, on the same deck as the dining-room and but a short distance from it. When I reached the office I sent for Miss Case, who was with me only for a few minutes when she herself went to call Colonel Worthington. It was then that his dead body was discovered."

There was a moment's silence. Professor Cross's thin ascetic lips moved mechanically.

"That," he said, "was very neat."

"Yes, very neat." A sneer twisted Jack Spencer's face. "Sounds like he had written it down and memorized it."

"There is no need for sarcasm, Mr. Spencer," returned the doctor, his voice well under control. Only his eyes betrayed his anger. "Perhaps you have a reason for blocking me."

"Just what do you mean by that?"

It was the doctor who was tantalizing now.

"You'll know soon enough. Will you or will you not tell us where you were from one to four-thirty today?"

"Hell, why shouldn't I?" Well-manicured fingers played with a perfectly trimmed mustache. "The sand storm was over around one, wasn't it? Just about that time I was having highball number two in the smoking room. I had to go get my first one for the Arabs were too busy keeping the boat afloat to bother with mere passenger needs."

"Where were you between the time you left the smoking room for a drink and the time you returned to it?"

"I thought you were only interested in knowing what we were doing and thinking and saying from one o'clock on. I went for the drink around twelve-thirty or a little after." He was being decidedly unpleasant.

"Is there any reason why you don't want to answer my question? I rather fancy there is." Dr. Bradshaw was being unpleasant too.

"By God, if I had my way about it you'd lose your job right now. How dare you use that tone to me?"

"How dare you refuse to answer questions when three murders and a jewel robbery may be laid at your door?"

"That's what you're trying to do—trying to pin this business on me. Well, you'll have a hard time doing it."

Dr. Bradshaw was idly fingering the handle of the only gun.

"Do you intend answering me or am I wasting my time?"

"You're wasting your time all right, but I'll call your bluff and answer your question. When I left the crowd at twelve-thirty I went as straight to the bar as I could go. I say this because I had to feel my way, the lights being off and the sand so thick and blinding I couldn't see a hand before me. When I reached the bar I mixed a highball and sat at one of the tables drinking it. It was fairly cozy there and quiet, so I didn't hurry to leave. Finally I poured myself another pony and came back with it to this room."

"What time was that?"

"I didn't look at my watch but I think it was around one o'clock."

"Do you mean to tell me you sat in the bar alone for half an hour?"

"I do."

Dr. Bradshaw's blue eyes seemed to protrude further and further.

"It's not necessary for me to say that I don't believe you, is it?"

"It's not necessary for you to say a damn thing."

"Was anyone here at one o'clock?"

"No one but Jimmie Bean."

"How long did you stay in here?"

"Until the luncheon gong sounded. One of the Arabs showed up with some drinks and Jimmie and I had a couple apiece while we played chess."

"Did you go down to lunch together?"

"We did."

"Did you notice Colonel Worthington as you went by him on the deck?"

"I think so." His words were very careless. "I rather think Jimmie spoke to him."

"Do you remember whether he received any answer?"

Jack Spencer hesitated for the fraction of a second. "I am under the impression he didn't."

"And after lunch, what did you do?"

"I went to my room and stayed there until I heard a commotion in the hall. Naturally, I went out to see what was up and heard that Charlie Worthington was dead."

"Then what?"

"I think I enjoyed a few breaths and words before I retired again to my boudoir."

Heavy, loaded sarcasm in an already stifling atmosphere.

"Did you hear any noises just before Miss Singlefoot screamed?"

"I don't remember."

"If someone had been walking softly in the hall, would you have heard him?"

"I might."

"You can't be sure?"

"No."

"It strikes me that you were sticking close to your room."

"Does it?"

"Yes. Was there any particular reason for your doing so?"

"Yes, damn you, there was."

"Is it a secret?"

"No, I was packing. I wanted to be ready to leave this lousy boat at the first opportunity."

"You weren't thinking of leaving us too suddenly, were you?" Dr. Bradshaw smiled for the first time, a disagreeable sort of a smile.

"You know what I mean—as soon as the authorities take charge at Assuan." He glared at the exasperating man. "And that can't be too soon to suit me."

"Nor me," agreed the doctor, and turned to Jimmie Bean.

"I understand that you were in the room with Mr. Spencer until lunch time."

"That's right."

"And after you left the dining-room, where were you?"

"In the smoking room until one of the Arabs breezed in and said Colonel Worthington was dead. I helped you carry him downstairs, you know."

"Where were you when Miss Singlefoot screamed?"

"On the lower deck, watching the poling."

"Jack Spencer says he thinks you spoke to Colonel Worthington on your way to lunch. Did you?"

"Yes, I did."

"What did you say?"

"I don't remember exactly. Something like 'soup's on' or 'come join the bread line.'"

"Did he answer you?"

"No, he didn't."

"Weren't you surprised at that?"

"Aw, I never thought anything about it. You know how crabby these Englishmen are." Jimmie blushed furiously, "Sort of quiet and all that," he amended quickly as he remembered that Dr. Bradshaw was also English.

"I understand," said the doctor, and turned to Miss Singlefoot. "What did you do after I left your cabin at one-thirty?"

"Now, let's see," she twisted her long angular body forward, "if I remember rightly I went up to the card room to get a handkerchief I left there this morning. It was a linen one I bought in Florence before I came to Egypt. It had real lace on it and so, of course, I didn't want to lose it. I wouldn't ordinarily be using such nice handkerchiefs in the morning but the truth of the matter is I'm running low on plain ones." She smiled at the doctor who was listening impatiently to her long recital. "What with all this excitement I need more than usual," she explained.

"Yes, yes," returned the harassed man, who had caught the pleased "I told you so" expression on Professor Cross's face. "What did you do when you found the handkerchief?"

"Oh, I didn't find it, that was the trouble. I asked Jimmie and Mr. Spencer if they'd seen it; they were playing chess at one of the tables, and said they hadn't, so I went to the smoking lounge and sure enough, there it was on the floor by that long settee."

"And then you went down to the dining-room," urged the doctor. This woman was enough to vex a saint. The chances of stopping her were slight once she got started.

"Well, yes. Sophie came into the room about that time and suggested we go to lunch, so we did."

"Did you by any chance pass Colonel Worthington's chair on the way down?"

"No, I should say not. Why, I'd been a nervous wreck if I had."

"Why?"

She stared at the doctor.

"I could never pass a dead person without quaking in my shoes," she said solemnly.

"But how did you know he was dead?"

Miss Singlefoot was obviously upset. She glanced at Mona helplessly.

"I didn't at the time, but if I had known it—that's what I really meant. Didn't you say he died at one o'clock?"

"I said he had been dead around two hours when his body was discovered." The doctor's voice was heavy with weariness. Miss Singlefoot was either very stupid or very clever. He couldn't tell which. He was too tired to find out what she was really trying to say. He gave it up.

"I suppose you went to your cabin after lunch."

"Why, yes, I did. I thought it would be a good time to pack. It was a job too. You see, I didn't know just what kind of weather we'd find up here so I brought all my clothes. I think there's nothing quite as uncomfortable as being in a place without proper clothes. I remember once going to Atlantic City in the summer time and carrying only cool weather clothes and, would you believe it, the thermometer never got below ninety in the daytime." She paused to let the astounding information sink in.

Dr. Bradshaw grasped his opportunity.

"Thank you so much, Miss Singlefoot. That covers everything nicely. You went to your room to pack after lunch, stayed there until three o'clock and sat beside Mrs. Worthington until the disturbance at four-thirty."

"But I—" she began eagerly.

"Some other time," interrupted Dr. Bradshaw. "We must go on now. How about you, Professor Cross? Can you help us any?"

That scholarly gentleman smiled slyly at the doctor. "Won't you admit you're wrong?" he asked. "This questioning has been futile, hasn't it?"

Dr. Bradshaw looked at Mona, who returned the pudgy and much abused little man's nod.

"Miss Case and I think we've learned a lot," he said. "Certain people's characters have been disclosed."

"You're right at that," agreed Professor Cross. "They have."

"Where were you," asked Dr. Bradshaw, becoming suddenly abrupt, "during that hour before lunch?"

The answer was a complete surprise.

"I was sitting on the deck reading."

"On the deck? Whereabouts?"

Professor Cross smiled a frosty smile.

"There were three chairs," he said, "on the west deck. One was in the bow, the other two were placed side by side, near the middle of the boat. I occupied the chair next to the one in which Colonel Worthington met his death."

Dr. Bradshaw didn't know quite how to proceed.

"I suppose you and the deceased had some conversation together?"

"Some."

"Was he disturbed over anything? Did he impress you as a man who feared an impending death?"

"Not at all. I had lent him a book to read and he seemed to be interested in it. By that I mean he preferred to read rather than carry on a conversation with me."

"I understand," said the doctor, and hastened to ask his next question. "How long did you sit on deck?"

"Until the luncheon gong sounded."

"What then?"

"I suggested to Colonel Worthington that we go down to lunch."

"And he declined, giving indigestion as the reason?"

"Yes, he said the food was too bad for even a soldier to eat."

"And you agreed with him, I suppose."

"Quite so, I did. Then I called to Mr. Amory here and we went down together."

"Mr. Amory? Where was he?"

"Sitting in the third chair."

"Was he there all the time?"

"Yes, he was there when I went out around twelve o'clock."

"Colonel Worthington was alive, I take it, when the two of you left the deck?"

"He was."

"And after lunch, what did you do?"

"I went to the smoking lounge where I stayed until almost three o'clock, when the sun made it unbearably hot. I started down to my cabin and on the way came upon Miss Case standing beside Colonel Worthington's dead body."

"So it was the sun that drove you out?" The slow words were a challenge.

"Perhaps—or if you believe in such things, a premonition of evil."

"I don't," said the doctor shortly.

Someone was knocking on the door—it sounded more like a clenched fist than the knuckles of a hand. "I wonder—" he began, but the words died in his mouth.

Jane Davet, Celia's English maid, had opened the door and was standing on the threshold.

"I must see you, sir," she said, the words tumbling over each other, "right away. I can't wait any longer. I've got to tell."

She stopped suddenly, her eyes riveted on Jack Spencer's face. The sneer that she saw there brought a look of fear into her eyes.

"I've got to tell," she repeated weakly, her voice a thread of despair.

CHAPTER XXX
WHAT STOPPED THE BOAT?

"What's troubling you?" encouraged the doctor.

Jane Davet sat before him in an uncomfortable straight chair. Her back was to Jack Spencer.

"It's a long story, sir," she said.

"We have plenty of time," he returned with dry humor.

"It began in Cairo after Miss Lawton engaged me."

"What do you mean, 'engaged you'? Haven't you been with Miss Lawton a long time?"

"Oh, no, sir. Only since Cairo. Her French maid married quite suddenly, sir, and left her. That's how I happened to be here. She engaged me through an English agency about a month ago."

"Why didn't you tell me this before?" he asked sternly.

"I never thought it mattered, sir."

"Go on."

"I had been with her a week when he first spoke to me."

"He? Whom do you mean?"

"Jack—that is, Mr. Spencer, sir."

"What did he have to say?"

"Nothing much, sir. He said I reminded him of someone he knew back in England, so we got to talking about London and Exeter. I come from Devonshire, you see. He liked it, too." She paused for a moment. Devon, beautiful Devon, so dear and so remote from this hot, sticky boat. "We got very friendly, sir," she concluded, her rather large nose red and twitching nervously. "That was the whole trouble—too friendly."

"You were going to tell us something, I believe," suggested the doctor gently.

Now that the time had come, Jane Davet was tongue-tied. She rubbed her palms together agitatedly and seemed to cower lower in the chair.

"If I had known it was murder, sir, I'd never have agreed to it. I thought it was only the jewels."

"What do you mean—murder?"

"Mr. Spencer, sir. He stole the jewels, then murdered Miss Lawton to shut her mouth. But, I swear, sir, I didn't know about the murder. It was only the jewels, sir, only the jewels."

Dr. Bradshaw looked over the woman's head to where Jack Spencer sat, calmly smoking a cigarette. If he was perturbed by this sudden accusation, he gave no sign. He met the doctor's gaze without a flicker of an eyelash.

"Ask the fool," he said coldly, "how much someone is paying her to tell this fairy tale."

"Oh, but it's true, every word of it. He did it, sir, as sure as my name is Jane Davet."

"Are you certain it is your real name?" taunted Jack Spencer. "Or for purposes known only to yourself is it an assumed one?"

She did not answer, and Dr. Bradshaw ignored the question completely.

"Tell us what you know," he said, "and be very careful to tell the truth." He glared over her head. "As for you, be quiet. I don't think she's lying."

Jack Spencer shrugged his shoulders and blew a smoke ring.

"*Cela ne fait rien*," he muttered softly.

Miss Singlefoot turned to Mona. "Is he swearing at her?" she whispered.

"He is right," Jane began bitterly, before Mona could answer her aunt's question. "I was a fool but I'm not one any longer. I might have known he couldn't really love me. I'm too plain." Her lips trembled but she did not hesitate. "The first day after we left Assuan he came to me and said he wanted to make a proposition. He admitted he was a jewel thief, and promised that if I'd help him get Miss Lawton's jewels he would marry me as soon as we got back to Cairo.

He said he loved me—" here her voice broke pitifully—"and no one else had ever told me that. I believed him and agreed to do whatever he suggested. He asked me to describe where she kept the jewels, when I was off duty and the times that Miss Lawton was likely to be out of her cabin. Everything was arranged and then suddenly, the next night he came to me and said he had decided not to rob Miss Lawton, that we must forget the whole affair. I was glad of it and I told him so. It was then he told me he couldn't marry me. I accused him of loving someone else—Mrs. Worthington maybe. He swore he loved only me but that he didn't have enough money to marry. He said he had a lot of gambling debts and if they weren't paid he'd get into trouble. Then he asked me to meet him on Wednesday night, the night before Miss Lawton died. I went to the meeting place, which was that dark corner near the hatchway. He never came. I realized then he had been leading me on the whole time." She clenched her hands at the memory. "Just leading me on," she repeated sadly.

"What time did he tell you to meet him?"

"Ten o'clock."

There was conviction in Mona's steady voice, as she turned to the doctor. "He makes a date with Jane at ten so she won't by any chance be in her mistress's room. Then he intends to sneak down when Celia is upstairs. His plans are almost upset, though, when the usually wide-awake Celia decides to retire early. He is saved by her going to my cabin to borrow some glasses. If I remember rightly, he urged her to get them that night and not wait until the next morning. He found out from Jane where Celia kept her jewels, so it didn't take him long to steal them."

"What makes you think Mr. Spencer took the jewels, Jane?" asked the doctor.

"When I discovered the case was missing this morning I was surprised and afraid. I immediately thought of Jack, of course. He had lied to me." A world of bitterness was in her words. "You see," she explained, "I know he had been in her cabin because I found his scarf pin beside the dresser. It was not there the day before." She drew a small diamond pin from her pocket. "This is what frightened me so this morning. I was afraid you had seen me pick it up."

"No," said the doctor slowly, "I didn't see you. But why should Jack Spencer kill Miss Lawton? Had he ever suggested such a thing?" He was watching the maid closely.

"Yes, when we were planning to steal the jewels. I was worried for fear something would go wrong and Miss Lawton would catch him at it. He just laughed and said that nothing could stop him, that if she caught him in the act it would be her last catch, for her throat would feel something stronger than a necklace."

"That," said Jack Spencer, his words hard and cold as winter sleet, "is a lie."

"Then the rest is true?" asked the doctor quickly.

Spencer was lighting a cigarette.

"No, none of it is true," he answered deliberately.

"But why deny only part of it?"

"The rest of her tale is amusing and quite evidently a put-up affair. I can laugh at being accused of theft, but not murder. That's going too far."

Dr. Bradshaw's glance wavered between the shrinking English maid and the confident American. There was a ring of truth in the man's words and a deserved indignation, yet why should Jane come forward so willingly with this accusation if it had no foundation?

"You must have thought you loved Mr. Spencer if you'd agree to help him steal. What has changed you? Why have you decided to betray him?"

"I loved him because I was foolish enough to believe he loved me. But when he broke our tryst and stole the jewels on the sly I realized he had tricked me from the beginning." She bent her awkward body forward. "I come of honest folks," she said, "and we draw the line at murder. Since this morning I've been thinking hard. If they arrested Mr. Spencer for murder I'd be in it, too, and I decided to tell the truth. I don't want to go to jail for something I didn't have anything to do with."

"Would you swear to the truth of what you've just told us?" asked the doctor.

"Oh, yes, sir. It's all the God's truth." She seemed to be relieved and unafraid now that she had gotten the secret off her chest.

Jack Spencer looked the doctor straight in the eye.

"And I'd swear," he said slowly, "that it was all a lie. My word on oath would be better than hers in any court."

"But suppose your conversation with Jane this morning during the sandstorm was overheard? What then?"

Jack Spencer stared at him in surprise.

"You were standing outside of Miss Singlefoot's cabin," explained the doctor. "Your words drifted in with the sand."

"Miss Singlefoot is a prying old woman. However, at that, our conversation was harmless. We were simply discussing the murder, my gambling debts and robbery. If Miss Singlefoot heard everything we said she'll remember that I denied it all."

"What did you mean when you said, 'I had to do it'?"

Jack Spencer smiled an assured smile.

"I was talking about breaking the date. I explained to Jane that I couldn't get away to meet her. Our little affair," he was positively smirking, "had to be *sub rosa*. God knows I didn't care about the rest of you being on to my flirting with a common servant, harmless as it was."

Jane flinched at his callousness.

"All I've said is true, sir," she was crying softly. "It's true, so help me God."

"You poor thing," murmured Miss Singlefoot, almost in tears herself. "I believe you."

"This is all tommy-rot," said Jack Spencer. "I admit I shouldn't have played up to a stupid maid, but I did. The boat was so dull and, well, one must do something for amusement. When I saw my mistake I tried to get out of it as quickly as I could. It didn't work and as a consequence comes this unfortunate mess. However, she can't prove any of these things. She may be hurt and angry and doing this on her own initiative or she may be paid by the real thief and murderer to cast suspicion on me. Whichever it is, there's no proof. The scarf pin, itself, was obviously planted. I can't remember when I first missed it. Anyhow," he concluded wearily, "they don't convict people even in Egypt on such evidence as she has concocted. I'm not worried."

He was right and everyone knew it. Criminal or not, the evidence against him was not adequate.

"There should be a law," snapped Miss Singlefoot, "which provides—"

But no one ever learned what amendment she had in mind to improve the statutes of the country, for at that moment the *Assuit* hit a mud bank. Chairs and people toppled over each other at the jar and the boat rocked dangerously for a moment, then stood still. Not a sound was heard except the muffled shouts of the Arab sailors.

"Why, even the engine has stopped," gasped the doctor. "That was a bad jolt. I'll have to go down and see what's wrong." He barked a command to the startled group. "You stay here until I come back."

"But really—" began Professor Cross, and was interrupted.

"I am leaving an Arab to see that you stay," continued the doctor. "Only Miss Case can come with me; that is, if she wants to."

He nodded at Mona, who was staring at Jack Spencer. She had been staring at him since Dr. Bradshaw spoke of the engine. For the first time a look of fear clouded his dark eyes, fear verging close to abject terror. What unknown threat did the engine room hold for him? There was one way to find out.

"Yes, I'm coming with you, Doctor," she said, and left the room, two conflicting ideas fighting for the supremacy of her reason—a small, hard object locked in her desk drawer and Jack Spencer's terror-stricken face.

CHAPTER XXXI
WITHIN THE WHEELS

"I don't understand it," said the doctor, brushing damp fingers across his tired eyes. "I don't see how this power control got in such a position." He stopped at a sudden thought. "Not unless someone pushed it. But no one was down here except the Arabs and they wouldn't meddle with it." He shook his head wearily. "No, I don't understand it."

"Do you mean," asked Mona thoughtfully, "that if this lever is suddenly pushed from high speed to zero that the motor is cut off?"

"Not necessarily," returned the doctor, "in fact, I think not at all. However, a severe jolt, such as we experienced when we hit the mud bank just now, coupled with the sudden shifting from maximum to minimum speed would in every instance kill the engine."

"Maybe one of the Arabs was nearby when we struck the bank and pulled the lever to prevent the engine from stalling."

Dr. Bradshaw shook his head.

"The jolt and the stopping of the engine were so close together as to be almost simultaneous. Someone must have had a hand on the lever at the time or—" his voice trailed off helplessly as he repeated for the third time, "I don't understand it."

Mona leaned over to peer down into the shiny black wheels and motionless pistons. It was queer. Someone or something had pushed the control lever. It couldn't have moved of its own accord.

"As soon as we are under way again I'll ask the sailors if any of them touched this thing. That's the only possible explanation, after all, and even then we're probably running against a blank wall." He wiped his oily hands on a limp handkerchief, and started slowly toward Mona's side of the engine. "I'm afraid," he said, pointing to the front of her skirt, "you've ruined your dress. It's a pity."

Mona looked down at the tan skirt she wore. There were two long black strips of grease across the front of it.

"That's funny," she said, "very funny."

She was thinking of something soft and white—of a pair of flannel trousers with two grease streaks across them. Someone else had leaned over the engine as she had been leaning. But why?

"It must have come off here." Dr. Bradshaw rubbed his hand across two of the rails. His fingers were covered with grease.

Mona said nothing. She stood gazing down into the machinery as if it hypnotized her. Suddenly she grabbed the doctor's arm.

"I think," she said, "I know who moved that lever. It was the thief."

"The thief?" Uncomprehendingly the doctor peered into the silent engine.

"Yes," Mona was measuring the distance from the iron rail and something buried deep between the wheels and shafts. "What we need," she continued in an excited voice, "is a long rod with a hook on it."

"Would one of the grapple hooks do?"

"Is that what the sailors use to hold the boat steady when we are tying up at the dock?"

"Yes. Let me get one."

He disappeared for a second around the corner of the stairway. Soon he returned with an iron bar, the end of which was curved to form an ideal grappling hook.

"Just the thing," said Mona, still not explaining what it was all about. She moved aside a little to let the doctor stand where she had been standing. "You'd better do this. Your arms are longer than mine. Lean forward to the left and look at the wall back of the big wheel. Do you see anything?"

Dr. Bradshaw leaned over as she directed, but saw nothing except a bare wall, shiny with grease, and with occasional bolts protruding from its slick surface.

"Sorry, I can't say I do."

"Don't you see something on the lower middle bolt?" She was almost appealing in her insistence.

He strained forward and then nodded his head.

"There is a bit of twine or dirty string around it."

"Swell," said Mona. "That's what I wanted the hook for. See if you can't get hold of it. Do please be careful, though, for I believe something is hanging under the machinery from that very piece of string."

The doctor took the iron rod and, leaning forward, made a great effort to insert the hook. He could not quite reach it, but Mona urged him on.

"We've got to get hold of the string," she said. "Please try again."

In a last attempt he exerted all his strength and finally succeeded. The weight that he felt pulling at the piece of iron surprised him. He lifted it up carefully so that it didn't catch in the machinery. A little brown bag, strangely heavy, was on the end of the string. His hands shook as he handed it to Mona.

"This is heavy enough," he said hoarsely, "to push the lever if it swung against it very hard. And that was a terrible jolt when we hit the mud bank."

Mona opened the brown bag and held up a lead paperweight

"This is what weighed the bag down. Whoever put it there wasn't taking any chances of its getting tangled in the engine."

"Yes," agreed the doctor, taking the weight in his hand. "Something of the sort was necessary to keep the bag perpendicular. What's in it, anyway?"

Mona smiled a twisted little smile.

"Don't you know?" she asked, and before he could say a word, went on: "Diamonds and pearls and emeralds which for the first time in their existence have done something useful."

"You mean they stopped the boat? Is that it?"

"Just partly. They pushed the lever, and in so doing helped us find them, the stolen jewels, as well as the person who put them there."

Dr. Bradshaw's blue eyes protruded further and further.

"But have we?" Apparently it was hard for him to believe.

"Yes," returned Mona. "These two little initials tell the story."

She lifted her thumb from a small square patch of embroidery inside the lining of the leather bag. It was a beautiful piece of needle-work just as one would expect to find on the belongings of a fastidious person. The elaborately entwined letters were strangely clear —J. S.

"Jack Spencer," gasped the doctor.

"Or John Stewart," returned Mona and smiled at the surprise on the startled man's face.

CHAPTER XXXII
ASK THE COOK

Two objects stood out on the doctor's cluttered desk. They were a brown leather bag and a pair of white flannel trousers across the front of which ran two black streaks.

Jack Spencer no longer smiled. The knot of his pale green tie was loosened and had slipped around under his miserably wilted stiff collar. It had been a short interview but long enough to age him perceptibly.

"There's nothing else for me to do but admit it," he said, his eyes on the thin steel instrument that Dr. Bradshaw turned slowly in his hand. "I was the one who tried to get into Tom's cabin last night. He and Celia had the peculiar habit of writing each other notes even when they were in the same town. I knew they had had several little spats lately and I thought perhaps I might find in Tom's letter case an angry note from Celia. If the murderer weren't discovered, such a note could be used for blackmail purposes since it gives a motive for the killing and substantiates the theory of jealousy on Tom's part.

"That gadget you have in your hand is the one I used to get into Colonel Worthington's cabin this afternoon. I wanted to see if you had discovered the empty jewel case I planted there and if not I was going to put it in Tom's room." He tugged at his dapper mustache fiercely. "It was no use casting suspicion on Worthington, now that he was dead."

"No," returned the doctor dryly, "especially when you killed him." He seemed to be fascinated with the shining steel blade, for he kept turning it in his hand. "Do you have other such useful tools?" he asked, holding up the instrument, which looked like a palette knife.

Jack Spencer swallowed nervously and when he answered, his voice was that of an exhausted radio announcer.

"Yes, a very fine set of gentleman's tools."

"By that I suppose you mean ordinary burglar's tools." The doctor's voice was harsh and unpleasant. "Where have you kept them?"

"My tools could never be called ordinary," said the tired man. "The most beautifully and skillfully wrought burglar's set in all Europe is hidden in the false bottom of my Gladstone bag. If you hadn't searched me just now and found the jigger, no one would have known about it, though." He shrugged drooping shoulders. "However, it's no matter. I don't suppose I'll have an opportunity to use them for quite a while."

"No, not for a very long while, if ever." Dr. Bradshaw proceeded with his questioning. "When did you steal the jewels?"

"On the night before Celia was murdered while she was in Miss Case's room. Jane had told me where she kept her jewels. My flirtation with the maid had been for this purpose. When I got the jewels I put them, along with the tools, in the bottom of my bag. After Celia died and you pronounced it murder I became frightened, for I knew all the cabins would be searched. My one desire was to get those jewels as far from me as possible. Finally I thought of the engine room and that explains why I put the lights out of commission last night. I didn't want to run the chance of having anyone see me hide them." He looked down on his clasped hands and added bitterly, "I'd never have been caught, either, if I had gotten rid of those trousers. It was the damn stripes that gave me away."

"Yes," returned Mona, "the stripes on your trousers told me that you had leaned over the engine rail. The initials on the silk bag told us the rest."

"Why in the world," asked the doctor, "didn't you think of the initials?"

Jack Spencer smiled sadly. "Probably, after all, it was my conceit that made me forget them. Especially as I didn't really think the bag would ever be discovered."

"And now," said Dr. Bradshaw, his eyes luminous and moist from the heat behind his thick glasses, "tell us how you went about the murders."

"The murders?"

"Yes, the three murders you committed."

"Before God, I don't know a thing about them."

"That," retorted the doctor shortly, "is what you said when Jane Davet accused you of stealing the jewels. When we get proof of the murders, you'll confess them, too."

"You'll never get proof." Jack Spencer's long fingers were rubbing his neck nervously. "Just what are you going to do about me? Lock me up somewhere?"

"Yes, I'm going to lock you up and put a guard around the cabin. You are no longer a passenger. You are a prisoner, a thief and murderer."

"Why are you so anxious to have me branded as the murderer?" His tone was insistently curious. "Do you have a personal reason for not wanting the police to search for the real assassin, who masquerades under another name?"

Mona, watching the scene with unveiled excitement, detected a tinge of sarcasm in that weary voice.

"Bosh," snapped Dr. Bradshaw. His manner had a mild sort of triumph about it. "I would like a signed confession from you," he said, the pupils of his eyes like needle points. "A signed confession before I lock you up."

Mona shrank involuntarily at the mockery on his face and in his voice. He was like a spider taunting a crippled fly. He had changed before her eyes these last few days. She hated to see it, just as she hated everything connected with the ill-fated trip. She was so tired of it all that even if she happened to discover the murderer she would dislike turning him over to the Egyptian police. Perhaps he would commit suicide. That would be easier on everyone.

"I think I'll go now." She stood for a moment looking at the two men—the one fat, ruddy cheeked and gloating, the other, slim, haggard and helpless. "I'll be in my room if you should want me."

Dr. Bradshaw followed her to the door.

"Even though I am convinced we have the murderer here, I might be wrong. You must continue to be careful," he warned her, lowering his voice but not enough so that Jack Spencer did not hear and, as a result, smile sardonically at the thoughts the words provoked.

"Oh, I'll be careful," returned Mona and walked slowly down the hall. She could feel the doctor's eyes following her, boring into her tense back. Then came the click of a latch. He had closed the door. It was her signal and without a backward look she ran down the stairs and to the half-landing which led to Dr. Bradshaw's sleeping cabin. The door was unlocked and she did not hesitate to enter and close it behind her.

The room was as commonplace as Mona's actions were unusual and irregular. She searched it systematically but found absolutely nothing to warrant her trouble.

"There's not a darn thing here," she muttered to herself in a disgusted tone. "Even the waste-paper basket proves to be a flop. Nothing in it but dried dirt and some leaves." She stopped in surprise at her own thoughts. "Dried dirt and leaves," she repeated, her eyes fixed on the bookshelves. For a full minute she stared, as if fascinated by the brightly colored volumes that stood side by side beckoning challengingly to her. A book bound in dark green leather finally drew and held her attention. Without further hesitation she removed it from its place and turned to the light. The little dark streak that ran the length of the white paper edge interested her. She opened the book at that place and read with interest the written page.

"Humph," she said in a recklessly loud voice, "a treatise on the asp family. The page is worn and soiled, too."

She shut the book with a snap, put it carefully back on the shelf and slipped out of the room. Descending the stairway in almost a run she bumped into Jimmie.

"Where are you going in such a rush?" he asked, his teeth gleaming white in the dim light.

Mona was surprised at herself for wasting precious time in answering him.

"I'm going down to the servant's quarters," she said, "to ask the waiter what he serves each one for breakfast."

Then she continued on her way, leaving behind her an astonished Jimmie Bean.

CHAPTER XXXIII
THE GLOVES FIT

The information Mona obtained in the kitchen convinced her that she should no longer postpone her visit to Sophie's cabin. It was with a feeling of suppressed excitement that she turned the knob of the door and found it unlocked. Everything on the boat was unlocked now that Dr. Bradshaw claimed to have the murderer safely put away.

She could hear footsteps on the stairs. A close observer would have said they belonged to a heavy man peculiarly light on his feet. As Mona closed the door she caught a glimpse of Dr. Bradshaw creeping cautiously down the steps. She smiled to herself. She was taking no chances.

Sophie appeared to be sleeping quietly, an untroubled look on her full lips. Sleep had taken her far from ghastly reality.

A board creaked loudly beneath Mona's weight as she tiptoed to the dresser. She looked apprehensively at Sophie, who did not stir.

Ah, there were the gloves in the top drawer. A big pile of them, worn ones mixed with fresh ones. Mona did a strange thing. She tried on all the worn ones. One pair was fully four sizes too large for her. She held them up to the light and examined them carefully. Beige cotton gloves, very heavy with the seams sewed on the outside.

Not a sound broke the stillness of the room. It was enveloped in the quietness of death.

"Just why are you interested in those gloves, Miss Case?" The words were like the sudden popping of a pine coffin in a dry mausoleum.

Mona whirled to find Sophie, an odd smile on her face, standing behind her. Her getting out of bed and crossing the floor had been noiseless.

"I was wondering," said Mona thoughtfully, "whom these gloves belonged to." She handed them to Sophie, who pulled on the right one. It was obviously much too big.

"I'm afraid I can't help you." She shook her head. "You can see they don't belong to me. They are at least two sizes too large."

"Yes," returned Mona, "I can see that. Perhaps you will know whether they belonged to Colonel Worthington. If they belonged to him that would explain what they are doing in your dresser drawer."

"Charlie, when he wore cotton gloves, always wore thin ones. He used to say that thick ones made his hands perspire." She looked down at the gloves and wriggled her fingers in the empty spaces. "No, I don't think they belonged to him."

"May I sit down?" asked Mona, dropping into a straight chair by the closed door. She heard a slight noise just outside and wondered vaguely if the doctor could hear all the conversation. He was evidently trying to, for the door fairly bulged from his pressure.

"Certainly," returned Sophie, slipping into a beautiful silk negligee, "though I must ask you to leave soon for I have my packing to do. If we reach Assuan tonight, and I suppose we shall, I'll have to begin on it before long."

"Yes, I feel sure we'll dock tonight. By the way, did you hear any of the excitement we had this afternoon?"

"Excitement? No, the sedative Dr. Bradshaw gave me was very potent and I didn't wake up until now. What happened? Has the—er—murderer been discovered?"

"Not officially, though Jack Spencer has confessed to stealing the jewels."

Mona was not able to tell from Sophie's expression whether she was surprised at this or not. Since the first outburst at her husband's death the woman's face had become an impassive mask.

"What do you mean 'not officially,' Miss Case?" There was no anxiety in the question, only curiosity and the natural interest of a chance participant in an unfortunate affair.

"I would like to talk to you, seriously," said Mona, looking the dead man's wife straight in the eye.

Sophie returned Mona's stare with unflinching blue eyes.

"You can't mean you suspect me of killing my own husband?" Her tone of voice implied doubt if not positive disbelief in the possibility of anyone's thinking so.

"No, I don't suspect you, but I think you can help me by letting me talk it over with you." Mona drew a deep breath and hesitated for a second. She was listening intently for the sound of heavy breathing outside the door.

"You see," she continued, "I don't trust anyone, and since you are now personally interested in discovering the murderer, I feel I can be frank with you. I don't suspect you now, but I did at noon today." A strange emphasis lingered on her words. "And early this morning, I am sorry to say, Dr. Bradshaw and I thought Colonel Worthington was guilty."

"Not Charlie!" The words were almost a sob. "Charlie wouldn't have harmed a fly."

"Was he especially particular about brushing his hair?" asked Mona, suddenly remembering what Tom had said about the Englishman's appearing in the middle of the night with his hair combed.

"I don't understand what connection that has with all the rest," returned Sophie in evident perplexity, "but I certainly can answer your question. A man never lived who was as fastidious as Charlie about his hair. It all comes of his having been a soldier and required to be in perfect uniform on a minute's notice. In India, sometimes in the middle of the night there would be an alarm and the whole regiment would have to be fully dressed and ready for action within five minutes after they were awakened. That's where Charlie got the habit, though he was naturally particular about his appearance."

Sophie didn't seem to mind talking about her husband. In fact, she appeared to enjoy it. Mona reflected that deep and sudden grief affects people in many different ways.

"Colonel Worthington, before he died, spoke of being forced to leave India and the army on account of some disease. Would it be asking too much if I inquired from what malady he suffered?"

"I don't know myself exactly what it was. Some sort of tropical fever, though. Poor Charlie suffered so from insomnia, which was a permanent result of it. Often, he'd sit all night reading because he couldn't sleep."

"And I suppose if he found he couldn't sleep, and got up to read, he'd brush his hair from habit, thinking, perhaps, he'd be up all night?"

"Why, yes, that's exactly what Charlie would do—I mean, would have done." Sophie's voice broke the merest trifle. "But why do you ask such questions? And what made you think that I, of all people, was the murderer?"

"Today at noon," said Mona slowly and gravely, "I came to the conclusion that the murderer was one of two people. Either you or Dr. Bradshaw."

"Dr. Bradshaw?" gasped Sophie, while Mona held up a long brown forefinger to her mouth in warning. "Not so loud," she almost whispered it. "Someone might hear you."

There was a distinct noise at that moment in the hall. The listener must have been upset at what he heard. Sophie didn't seem to notice. She was apparently wrapped in her own thoughts.

"A great deal depended on who owned those cotton gloves." Sophie looked down in amazement at her gloved hand while Mona continued in the same calm fashion. "When you tried on the gloves I no longer suspected you."

"Why did you ever suspect me? And why Dr. Bradshaw?" This was a different Sophie from the hysterical woman of the middle afternoon.

"I had my first suspicions of the doctor after a casual conversation with Tom. His description of John Stewart made me think he might be the doctor in disguise. Dr. Bradshaw is of the same height and general coloring as Celia's cousin. Now, no one has seen him for four or five years, maybe more. He could have dyed his hair, put on weight, and shaved his mustache. Then, of course, wearing those thick glasses would alter his appearance perceptibly, and sometimes one cannot distinguish the Bostonian accent from the English."

Mona glanced toward the door. Dr. Bradshaw, if he could hear everything that was said, was certainly getting an earful. And not a very pleasant one at that, but then, eavesdroppers seldom hear nice things about themselves. It's the penalty they pay for satisfying their curiosity.

"But what about me? How did I fit in?"

"I'll tell you why I suspected you. The whole affair hinges together. Piecemeal information and clues pointing to you led me finally to Dr. Bradshaw's cabin. From there I got the clue that practically settled the whole affair, with but a few loose ends." Mona glanced at her watch. "I will have to hurry," she said, "but I really must tell you the elaborate case I worked up against you. Part of it was pure supposition, I admit, and a great deal merely circumstantial evidence, both of which eventually led me to the discovery of the real criminal. Are you interested?"

"I am bound to be interested now that Charlie is one of the victims." Sophie leaned back in her chair, the frilly blue negligee emphasizing the first faint glow of color in her cheeks.

Lines of age were visible on her neck and under her eyes. Unconsciously the strain was telling on her—the strain of her husband's death and the long absence from a beauty parlor, with its expensive and elaborate facials.

"Thirty years ago," began Mona in a clear voice that was calculated to penetrate the thin wooden door and enlighten the fat little doctor, strangely anxious to know what was happening on the other side, "two children played together in a small New York town. One was the daughter of a wealthy banker and business man, while the other's father was a doctor struggling for existence in a place oddly full of older and more experienced physicians. I have a feeling that the banker's daughter had lots of playthings, pretty dresses and a great deal of attention, while the less fortunate doctor's child had none of these. On top of it all the banker's daughter possessed a rare beauty that far eclipsed that of the other little girl. At an early age jealousy sprang up between them, jealousy which instead of diminishing, increased with the years. When the time came for the two to go off to college the rich girl went to a fashionable eastern school and the poor girl went into training in a New York hospital to be a nurse. After a year of this the doctor died and left his daughter a bit of money or something of the sort happened, and she gave up nursing to take dancing lessons. Being pretty and a natural dancer, she soon got a job on the stage." Mona stopped for a minute. She heard a stealthy movement in the hall. Dr. Bradshaw was either getting restless or was so interested he had forgotten himself. Sophie opened her eyes.

"Go on," she said in a thin, tired voice, "I'm still interested." Her white lids closed again.

"This is the purest supposition, but I rather imagine that the childhood jealousy between the two had not been lost in the few years' separation. The rich woman lived in New York during the time the other was gradually becoming a famous actress. Perhaps the rich one met some of the actress's admirers, shall we say, and they fell for her. Perhaps one who was a particular friend of the actress deserted her for the exotic and wealthy banker's daughter. Then suddenly an Englishman visited America, went to Ziegfeld's show, saw the actress, became infatuated with her and proposed marriage. She didn't hesitate long for she realized that being almost thirty, her dancing days would soon be over. For the past two years she had lived with a newspaper man named John Stewart. Growing tired of the arrangement, he had thrown her over for a younger and blonder celebrity. The Englishman thought her innocent and naïve, he was supposedly rich, she had nothing to gain by staying in America, so she married him."

Sophie broke in.

"You are a journalist, I understand, Miss Case. You should succeed at it, for your imagination is very vivid and in most instances hits the mark. But where does Celia come into the picture?"

"I remember Colonel Worthington's saying she was your house guest in England this winter before you left for the Riviera and eventually Egypt. I imagine that it was then the jealousy between the two exceeded everything it had been in the past. Colonel Worthington fell in love with Celia and planned to meet her in Egypt later. However, from a conversation that was overheard, I think Celia resented his ardent attentions and planned to expose him on the very day she died."

Sophie had closed her eyes again and at this there was not a flicker of an eyelash. She couldn't be hurt or jealous, now that both Celia and Charlie were dead.

"And the next chapter to the story requires even more imagination. However, something of this sort happened in, say, Paris. Sophie is coming out of the Ritz one day when she runs into John Stewart, her former lover. He is evidently not on the 'up and up' as Sophie apparently is. He asks her about herself, and she tells him that she and her husband are on their way to Egypt and that Celia Lawton will be there, too. John Stewart becomes quite excited at this news and asks Sophie to meet him the next afternoon for tea at a small restaurant in Montmartre. She agrees, and at the Cafe Mere Catherine, John Stewart tells her he's broke, without a job and in desperate need of money. He has worked out a plan which he thinks infallible and warns Sophie that if she doesn't agree to it he will tell her husband that his wife was nothing but a common chorus girl who was promiscuous with her favors; in short, that she lived with him, John Stewart, for two years."

"A year and a half," interrupted the dead man's wife, "and the café was the Moulin Rouge, otherwise your supposition was correct. You are remarkable—very remarkable, and it's a shame."

"A shame? What do you mean?"

Sophie waved her right hand in a careless gesture.

"Oh, nothing. I'll tell you later. Do go on with your wild bold tale, if there's more to it. I admit John Stewart tried to blackmail me, but since poor Charlie had no money it wasn't any use. That's how it ended. I proved to John that after this winter we wouldn't be able to keep up a front, and as a consequence I had no money whatever to give him."

There had not been a sound from the hall for some time. Mona wondered if the listener were still there. It was a nerve-wracking situation. She glanced at her watch. She would feel safer after a few honest-to-goodness policemen were aboard.

"When I suspected you," she continued, "I had it figured out this way: John Stewart was blackmailing you, yes, but not for money. He asked you to kill Celia Lawton when you took this Nile trip together. I remember Celia said one day it was you who had suggested a *dahabeah* beyond the first cataract. At Celia's death John Stewart would inherit a fortune."

"And this fabrication," remarked Sophie abruptly, "is all wrong. You see it now?"

"I admit it was the wildest supposition, but it was just the beginning of the road. At the end of it I found the answer which was a terrible fact, not a chance guess."

"If John had suggested such a thing, I would have been in a bad situation. Charlie would have divorced me sure—with no alimony."

"Exactly." Mona thought she heard a chuckle. Dr. Bradshaw was still listening at the door. She wondered if he held the gun in his hand or conveniently tucked away in his pocket. It was all a question of time and she was fighting hard. Fighting for time with life itself in the balance.

"This whole story, so far," continued Mona, "is simply an accumulation of possibilities. The things that prompted me to piece them together are still not quite clear in my mind, though you are no longer a suspect."

"And what are these things?" Sophie's blue eyes were clear and piercing. She was more interested and willing to give her time than Mona had expected.

"You remember the night someone tried to strangle me in the dark on the way to my cabin? Well, just before that I had been in Dr. Bradshaw's office, discussing the murder. Someone overheard our conversation—someone dressed in white, sitting on the stairway. You wore a white dress that evening, and more important was the question of rings. The strangler's hands were soft and ringless. While I was being revived in the smoking lounge I noticed that the fourth finger on your right hand was red and a bit swollen, as if you had jerked off your ring hurriedly. That was the beginning of the suspicion."

"But everyone was in white, whether it was a dress, or linen suit or wrap. Even Professor Cross wore white socks, and as for the red finger, a mosquito bit me there and I had scratched it."

"Oh, I didn't say these were facts—just possibilities or coincidences. Dr. Bradshaw was a logical strangler, too. I had just left his office but he could have come up the west stairway and he knew I meant to investigate the murder to the best of my ability. His hands, unused to manual labor, are soft and they're certainly strong. So are yours, for that matter."

"Yes, they are strong," Sophie's eyes were no longer closed. All listlessness had disappeared. She may not have known that Dr. Bradshaw was listening intently at the door but she sensed the impending drama in the air. She was so interested, she had forgotten to remove the glove from her right hand.

"And then there was the matter of the emerald ring. You weren't wearing it at lunch today, and when I remarked about it you said it was safe in your cabin. You didn't say that the emerald had been lost, as I knew it had, for at that moment it was in my pocket. Naturally, I wondered why you lied about it. The thought came to me that you probably had no idea where you lost it and feared that if you spread the news everyone would hunt for the stone and perhaps it would be found in a suspicious place."

"Where was it found?"

"Just beneath the pantry window where the ice picks were kept."

"That's strange. It must have fallen out when I went to lunch."

"It couldn't have," returned Mona. "For you see I went into the dining-room before you did and that was when I found the emerald."

"Perhaps breakfast, then." Sophie's words were careless. "But why so much significance to the stone?"

"My conclusion was that you had lied about the emerald because you were afraid you had lost it while leaning over to get the ice picks inside the pantry. You didn't dare hunt for it since it was dangerous to be seen close to that spot." Mona drew a deep breath and glanced at the door. Was it her imagination or did she see it moving? It occurred to her to ask Sophie if there was a weapon concealed anywhere in the room. However, not wanting to startle her, she added instead in an apologetic tone, "You see, at lunch time I suspected you of the murder. I was fairly jumping at conclusions."

"Rather," said Sophie dryly. "But how about this explanation? On a boat where there is a criminal who both kills and steals one would naturally hesitate to advertise such a loss. The emerald was a very valuable stone. If the thief knew it was missing he might join in the hunt, and if he were the finder keep it. Now that Charlie had become so poor I couldn't afford to take the chance so I simply planned to keep quiet about it until we reached Assuan and then report the loss to the proper authorities."

"I get your point. It is a possible explanation and a kinder one."

"Yes. Much kinder."

A friendly smile lighted Mona's face.

"I'm sorry," she said simply.

"But where does Dr. Bradshaw come in? It must have been a blow when you discovered he was the murderer. However, I don't think anyone aboard will be terribly surprised for from the first I've heard several muttering about him."

"I have had a vague suspicion." Mona stopped a second to stare at Sophie, who in turn was staring at the door.

"I thought I heard a noise in the hall," she said, her voice even and scarcely audible.

"Oh, everyone is busy packing—I'm sure it couldn't have been anything. Probably some knocking in the engine. I didn't hear a sound of any kind, myself."

Sophie started to rise from her chair and Mona was galvanized into speech.

"I was the one who searched your room," she said, "and found nothing but a lot of bills and a telegram. That telegram was signed 'S' and was an appointment to meet someone in Paris. At the time I thought nothing of it but later in the light of my growing suspicions it was damaging, for 'S' stands for Stewart among other names. I remembered the telegram right after your husband's murder. My theory was, you see, that you killed Celia from jealousy and for fear of being exposed to your husband as, shall we say, a loose woman. You killed Abdu, the Arab, because he was blackmailing you for something he had discovered in your room. The torn bank-note in his hand told that story. You made an appointment to meet him at the head of the stairs, then stole up behind and stabbed him in the back of his neck as you handed him the bills. You would have known just where to strike from the fact that your father was a doctor and that you had had a nurse's training. The reason for killing your husband, whom you stabbed just before you went to Miss Singlefoot's cabin and suggested going to lunch, was not quite evident but I think this is a logical explanation. You never loved him, you married him to escape an eventual poverty. On the other hand, you had never ceased to love John Stewart. Probably he said that if you murdered

Celia and then got rid of your husband he'd marry you and you'd enjoy the money together. You had already committed two murders—a third would not have been hard—especially since there were two ice picks."

Mona, even though she felt the impropriety of it, couldn't refrain from the last remark.

"You must have thought me a terrible woman," Sophie said. "I'm glad you no longer think so."

"I still think you are a clever woman. But let me finish. Time is passing. This afternoon I had an opportunity to search Dr. Bradshaw's cabin. It didn't yield much except some dried dirt and leaves."

"What in the world could that have to do with the murder? I don't see the connection."

"You know, of course, that Celia was killed by an asp bite. Does that explain it?"

"No, I'm afraid it doesn't."

"Well, briefly, then, tell you. The murderer stole an overnight bag from my aunt on the day we left Assuan. The bag was returned with nothing missing but a soap box. Later the box was found with some caked dirt and leaves in it. That makes it easy to figure out why it had been stolen."

"To house the asp?"

"Exactly. Incidentally, I will say here that Jimmie Bean and I were in the house of Nusa, the snake-charmer, the night the murderer got the asps—and we saw him board the boat but we didn't recognize him either time. If you were the murderer you simply followed the directions of John Stewart and visited Nusa who probably had already received word of your coming. If Dr. Bradshaw were the murderer, getting the asp was simple. Having been on this boat for several years he would know Nusa well."

Mona was talking very fast now.

"This is how the murderer managed Celia's death. He concealed the viper in a large soap container in which there was a little sand, dirt and grass. Each morning he put in a small portion of an uncooked egg. I will explain the egg part later. On the morning of Celia's murder he drew on a pair of thick leather gloves, and on top of this a pair of heavy cotton ones. He turned on his reading light, which has a large bulb, and held the snake close under its heat for fifteen minutes. Then later in the confusion of mounting the donkeys, he slipped the snake, warm and sluggish from eating and from the intense heat, into the pocket of Celia's camel's hair coat. He thought that while Celia rode along with the crowd on the way to the tomb, she might put her hand in her pocket, disturb the snake and be bitten. If she should not do so, the snake would lie quiet in the warmth of her pocket, lulled to sleep by the swaying motion of the donkey's gait. Then later in the tomb she would ram her hand into her pocket. The murderer felt there would be no suspicion cast upon him for he would not be seen near Celia that morning, that is, not after everyone mounted their donkeys. It was mere coincidence, Celia's dying before the figure of Anubis, God of the dead, though quite a likely place since Anubis is seen in all tombs and in many temples."

"But the dried dirt and leaves you found in the doctor's waste-paper basket, isn't there a logical explanation? He might have gotten that on his shoes when we tied up to collect the vegetables the other day. The banks are muddy and there is some shrubbery close to the water's edge."

"You're right, he might have cleaned his shoes and the Arab servant in all the excitement failed to empty the basket. On the other hand, that might have been remnants of his preparation for Celia's murder. However, what I started to tell you is, I found a book on his shelf, entitled *Snakes of the World*, and in it was a page devoted to the habits and foods of asps. The line saying the sand viper lived chiefly off leaves and raw eggs interested me. In that line lay the secret of the murder. All wild supposition vanished. I had but to find out what passenger ordered uncooked eggs for breakfast."

"But I should think the murderer would hesitate to give such an order each day. No one eats raw eggs."

"Oh, that's easily explained. The cook said one of the passengers complained that the one-minute egg ordered was too hard and demanded that two raw eggs and a bowl of boiling water be brought to him each morning, saying he would heat them himself."

"I never thought of that," said Sophie, a trifle nervously. She had been restless since she heard the noise in the hall. A woman's intuition is a great ferret of dangers. It often sees through doors to listeners beyond.

Mona thrust her hands into her pockets.

"Thus the search ended with the cook," she said slowly. "So many times answers to hard questions come from lowly sources." Her fingers closed on two little black screws in her pocket. "Oh, I forgot to mention these." She held them out in her hand. "I found these on the floor of this cabin when I searched it. I wonder where they came from?"

"Why, I don't know." A frown darkened Sophie's face. She looked around the room as if searching for an explanation. Her eyes fell on a moving picture camera. She leaned over and picked it up. "They may have come from this. It's broken and Charlie was trying to fix it the other day."

She held the camera up and inspected the black leather sides.

"No screws missing from the outside. I'll open it up and see if they could have come from the inside."

But Mona was not listening to Sophie. She had seen the knob of the door turn several times as if the eavesdropper were about to invade the room and wanted to see if the door were unlocked. Mona's tense body was like a harp chord which was tuned too tightly and would pop at the slightest provocation. She was fascinated by the drops of moisture clouding the lens of the camera. They reminded her of a baby's breath. Sophie's gloved hand had unlocked the case. It cautiously disappeared inside and stayed there. Sophie's eyes were like a sudden frost—hard, brittle and unexpected.

"So you weren't surprised to find the gloves too big. They had to be to go over leather ones."

Mona felt her own eyes grow glassy. Sophie was speaking again, her words as frigid as her eyes.

"You are not much larger than Celia and this poor dear is so very hungry." She was holding a small but wriggling something in her gloved hand. She had doubled under the overly long fingers of the glove where she held the hissing asp.

"I stole that silly old Miss Singlefoot's soap box because at the last minute I thought two vipers instead of one might come in handy. And I was right." She stood up and smiled at Mona—a cruel knife-like smile.

"I was forced into this thing, but now that I'm here, and three others are decidedly missing—" her body was convulsed with laughter—"you might as well be the fourth. There is such a thing as knowing too much and being too clever."

Mona also had risen from her chair.

"Don't think I'm such a fool as to have come here alone. Dr. Bradshaw has listened to the whole conversation." She nodded her head toward the opened door where Dr. Bradshaw stood, a gun in his hand.

"I said I no longer suspected you." Mona's words came through frightened lips. "That was true, for after I talked to the cook and then discovered these gloves in your dresser drawer I knew you were the murderer, and that Dr. Bradshaw was not John Stewart, for he was back in Paris waiting completion of his plans."

Sophie's bare left hand closed over her gloved right one with its wriggling burden, and a slight moan escaped her lips. She sank down into her chair.

"There will be no need for the gun," muttered Dr. Bradshaw, and gingerly pulled open Sophie's clenched hand, which was already red and swollen. On the palm lay a sand-colored asp, mangled and broken.

AFTERWORD

A NOTE ON THE HORNED VIPER
Chad Arment

From mysteries like Rex Stout's *Fer-de-lance* (1934) or Arthur Conan Doyle's "The Adventure of the Speckled Band" (1892), to thrillers like John Godey's *The Snake* (1978), deadly snakes are commonly used to create an atmosphere of danger and suspense. For the reptile aficionado, however, the intersection of literature and herpetology is often cringe-worthy when fiction writers convey wildly inaccurate details about the behavior, biology, or temperament of living reptiles. Any snake enthusiast who peruses *Death Sails the Nile,* for example, will readily spot several false notes when it comes to the dreaded horned viper.

This might typically be overlooked by a mystery reprint publisher, but as a herp enthusiast myself (in fact, I named my publishing company after a favorite snake, the coachwhip), it feels necessary to add a couple corrections in postscript. (It would have been difficult to change the original text itself, as details were entwined in the clueing.)

First, no snakes include leaves in their diet. A few may eat raw eggs (bird or lizard), but most are strictly predators of smaller animals, the specific prey depending on the species. For the horned viper, *Cerastes cerastes*, of North Africa and the Middle East, the diet includes small vertebrates (lizards, rodents, and birds). They are ambush predators, lying half-buried in the sand until their unwary meal passes.

Second, horned vipers do not stab or envenomate with the pointed 'horns' situated just over each eye. Those are modified scales, and have no value as defensive or offensive weapons. The snake's venom is delivered through their fangs. It certainly is possible for untreated envenomation to be life-threatening, and the species is considered medically significant in its natural range (and within the herpetocultural community, as *Cerastes* is commonly kept by venomous snake enthusiasts).

Still, it is hoped that the reader enjoyed the story. Future mystery writers are strongly urged, however, to take the time to get their ophidian details correct. In a world of *Animal Planet* and the *National Geographic Channel*, future generations are learning about curious creatures all over the world, and will be quick to recognize errors. There are plenty of online resources today to help guide descriptive prose.

MURDER TAKES
THE VEIL

MURDER AT
ST. DENNIS

SISTER SIMON'S
MURDER CASE

THE MARGARET ANN HUBBARD
MYSTERY OMNIBUS

COACHWHIP PUBLICATIONS

CoachwhipBooks.com

COACHWHIP PUBLICATIONS
CoachwhipBooks.com

MEDORA
FIELD

WHO KILLED
AUNT MAGGIE?

COACHWHIP PUBLICATIONS
CoachwhipBooks.com

THE QUINNY HITE
MYSTERIES

CHINESE RED · HERE LIES THE BODY

RICHARD BURKE

COACHWHIP PUBLICATIONS
CoachwhipBooks.com

The Serpentine Club Investigates
Murder in Washington, D.C.

THE CAPITAL
MURDER

JAMES Z. ALNER

COACHWHIP PUBLICATIONS

COACHWHIPBOOKS.COM

THE
RUMBLE
MURDERS

Henry Ware Eliot, Jr.

COACHWHIP PUBLICATIONS
COACHWHIPBOOKS.COM

DEAD
WEIGHT
ADDISON
SIMMONS

www.ingramcontent.com/pod-product-compliance
Lightning Source LLC
Chambersburg PA
CBHW020627260626
47157CB00009B/3214